THE MARK OF THE BUTCHER'S NEPHEW

Jay Flagg

Flagg & Flagg Ministries

To an amazing God, an astounding Savior,
and lover of my soul, with gratitude.

To my wonderful wife and fellow student
of God's Word, with delight.

To my grandkids, Mya, Amelia, and Morgan,
who live everyday like one big adventure, with joy.

CONTENTS

INTRODUCTION

This story is a fictional account of the origins of the Gospel of Mark. It is my attempt to grasp the rich, thoughtful narrative of Christ's life that Mark, inspired by God's Spirit, left for the church.

In this story, through the mind of a fictional young man named Rufus, I attempt to unpack some of the historical and theological thinking that John Mark brought to his work. He stuffed the narrative with massive insight from the Old Testament, where the prophets foresaw a unique Messiah and a radical vision for God's people.

I am indebted to Rikki J. Watts, G. K. Beale, and Benjamin L. Gladd for their intense work unpacking the Old Testament story as it connects to the life of Jesus and the New Testament. I'm grateful for my scholar wife, whose insights are amazing.

Thank you also to the biblical imagination of Michael Card, whose commentary on Mark is so unique in its investigation of Jesus — God and man, and is grounded in deep study and thoughtful reflection, both things to which I aspire. James

Edwards and Ben Worthington inspire depth and awe in their commentaries. Thank you.

Along the way, Rufus's story will invite you to some side streets such as evangelism, Scripture memory (highlighting a well thought out and effective method recommended by Andrew M. Davis), ancient Roman culture, and a few other things. Enjoy.

This story is that — a story. It cannot replace careful and fervent study of the Scriptures. I have taken some huge liberties at places, but none I hope that would steer you from knowing Jesus.

If you're an average reader, you can read the entire Gospel of Mark in about 55 minutes. It's worth the time.

I have two goals in sharing this small novel. First, I would like to incite your imagination and reflection as it pertains to biblical studies. God's story begins in Genesis and rushes with purpose toward Revelation. It is a grand masterpiece. Second, please fall in love again and anew with Jesus, our Messiah and Savior. He is astounding and deserves more attention than we give him.

With gratitude,

Jay Flagg

"To know oneself is, above all, to know what one lacks. It is to measure oneself against Truth and not the other way around. And the first product of self-knowledge is humility."

— FLANNERY O'CONNOR

"Mark's genius lies not in telling a story about Jesus but in creating conditions under which the reader may experience the peculiar quality of God's good news."

— C. CLIFTON BLACK

KINDLING

The smoldering air kindled a new dread at the center of Rufus's world. With the sweltering saga unfolding around him, pressing into his young adult life in ways he'd never envisioned, something was changing, but he couldn't name it.

The smell of charred boards mixed with a sustained tenseness stoked a climate of hatred and mistrust. Routinely calm and collected, Rufus was swept up into a cauldron of emotion.

Rufus found himself front and center, and he wasn't keen about it. Resisting the urge to check out, he peered over the edge of his overcast confusion. Rufus's intense curiosity had always filled his brain with a thousand thoughts, but when yielding to troubling emotions, he could, without effort, implode.

This was a critical situation, and he recognized that.

Dark smoke grayed the horizon. In parts of the city,

fires continued burning; they had been for days and nights.

And now Rufus stood in the middle of his district's plaza with about thirty or forty people. He and Agnus had been walking across the plaza toward her mother's merchant cart when the confrontation began, leaving Rufus trying to make sense of the speedy change in their circumstances.

A voice broke through the dense smoke of his psyche.

"Rufus, are you afraid of dying?"

The voice with its question startled him. Agnus, Priscilla's daughter, was talking to him. They had been best friends since childhood and spent most of their spare time together.

"What? No. I never thought about it. I don't think like that," he said. The pit of his stomach did a cartwheel. The question disturbed him.

Agnus stared at him. He looked at her. Her eyes pierced him, probing with their brown gaze.

They were standing at the edge of the group. People were mumbling and complaining. Anger was brewing. Rufus didn't recognize anybody. The soldiers had herded them into the middle of the forum. This square, at the center of their district, served as a marketplace and political center for this section of Rome that Rufus called home.

Years earlier, city fathers had modeled this negligible area, surrounded by small public buildings and ornate colonnades, after the larger market at the center of Rome. With its carts, makeshift shacks, and throngs of people and animals, this square was a familiar place for Rufus.

Right now, Rufus found himself crammed together with a group of shoppers. A cohort of Roman soldiers surrounded them. The group of detainees could move neither forward nor back.

Rufus fleetingly bounced his gaze from Agnus. He watched a child clinging to his mother. Another lady was sagging under the weight of a large water jug. He wanted to help her, but he dared not move. A centurion stood in front, looking over the amassed group of people in the plaza's center.

"Is he looking for someone in particular?" Rufus wondered.

The centurion nodded, and the soldiers used their spears to shove the crowd closer together. The child cried. An elderly gentleman snatched the jar from the lady as she staggered. The soldier nearest stuck a spear into the man's face.

"Don't move."

The baby continued crying.

The crest of feathers on the helmet of the soldier in front of Rufus and Agnus frittered in the breeze. It signified the man's rank. His stature and manner further clarified that he was in charge.

"You there."

The centurion used the hilt of his sword and pushed Rufus, who stumbled back, almost falling. Only bumping into the others crowded into the space prevented him from toppling over.

"Yes, sir." Not even a second passed before Rufus answered him.

"Who's in charge here?" The centurion was staring right at him with piercing blue eyes. At six feet tall, Rufus stared right back at the man. "You?"

Rufus didn't understand the question, but he knew the centurion expected an answer.

"No."

"You're Jewish; aren't you?"

"Yes, sir." Rufus was scrambling to make sense of what was happening. He couldn't. He glanced at Agnus, who was still at his side, staring down.

Agnus's question unsettled him even more now. He seldom, if ever, thought about dying. He wasn't prone to fear. His uncle always encouraged him; he would say, "Live hard today."

Even if the centurion had been without his fellow soldiers, Rufus understood he was no match for the hefty fellow. Had one of his schoolmates or peers confronted him, Rufus would have puffed up his chest and pushed back. He felt no such impulse now.

The centurion looked out at the small crowd. He glared.

"This is an illegal gathering," he said. "You must

disburse. In the Emperor's name, I order you to clear the square."

He nodded to the other soldiers. They lowered their lances, releasing the pressure they had exerted on the group. He repeated his command, and it echoed throughout the plaza, having a stirring effect on everyone there.

Immediately, Rufus grabbed Agnus by the arm and directed her toward the edge of the square. People ran, the crowd vanished, and doors slammed. Rufus could taste the dust in the air.

Agnus shook free and grabbed Rufus.

"What about my mother?"

"Yes," Rufus said. "You're right. Follow me. We'll head out toward the aqueduct and come in the north entrance. We'll be near her cart for certain. I'm sure we can find her."

Rufus sped off with Agnus on his heels. The incident had created mayhem as everyone rushed to evacuate the square. Rufus and Agnus made their way to the alley next to the aqueduct. A glut of people and animals crowded the alleyway. It was apparent to Rufus that several hundred meters down the back street, a crowd was jamming the passage in front of them.

Rufus jumped to grab a beam protruding from the side of the stucco building. He missed. He jumped again. Catching the beam, he pulled himself up high enough to see over the crowd. After catching a quick glimpse, he dropped to the ground.

"It's your mother."

"What?" Agnus said.

"Your mother's cart is blocking the alley ahead. She must have started down the back way before the crowd. She's stuck."

Rufus grabbed Agnus's hand. He pressed his way through the gridlocked crowd.

"Excuse me. Excuse me. I can help."

They squeezed through the mob. As they approached the cart, they felt the press of the blockage as the throng pushed harder and harder to get through. The canvas covering of Priscilla's cart was visible over the people who were trying to get past.

Rufus elbowed through with Agnus in his shadow. Upon reaching the cart, Agnus pushed past Rufus and plunged into her mother. She pulled her in for a hug and began sobbing. Her mother gasped.

"Oh mother, we were so worried about you," Agnus said.

"My child, I'm fine. You know that I've seen much worse than a minor scuffle with the Roman Guard."

She turned from her daughter and glanced back at her small wagon blocking the alley.

"I'm much more concerned about my tents and bags." She looked at the ruddy young man looming over her. "Give me a hand, Rufus. Will you?"

"Of course," he said. At seventeen, almost eighteen,

Rufus was strong. Hefting slabs of meat in his uncle's butcher shop had built his physique, while the extra food afforded him at his uncle's table hid the muscles with a few extra pounds and slowed him a bit.

Rufus surveyed the situation. Avoiding the people walking toward her, Priscilla had guided the mule close to the side of the alley, forcing one wheel of the cart to lodge sideways in a well-worn rut. The press of the panicked crowd kept the mule from being able to pull it out.

Within moments of his assessment, Rufus had a scrap board under the wheel and some space around the mule. He nodded to Priscilla.

"Coax her muzzle toward the center of the alley. Do it with firm gentleness."

People made space. Priscilla obeyed. And the wagon rocked forward out of the channel.

"Oh," Priscilla sighed out loud. Keeping a gentle tug on the reins, she coaxed the mule as she eased her cart and cargo down the alleyway.

Agnus and Rufus fell in behind her and followed her back the way they came. Progress was slow until the crowd dissipated.

As they approached the *Via Appolonia*, Rufus stepped up alongside Priscilla.

"I need to help my uncle. Are you guys going to be all right?"

Priscilla nodded. "We will. Thanks so much, Rufus.

You're always so kind and good. You are very brave as well."

He blushed.

"We will see you when we gather next."

Rufus said his goodbyes to Agnus and turned down the street.

SEARING ANGER

Anger burned in the emperor's heart. He had no vent to accommodate it.

The fire had everyone in Rome talking.

It started early on the morning of July 19. The blaze broke out in a shop near the *Circus Maximus*, the mammoth stadium near the middle of the city. No one would say which shop, but rumors suggested it might have started in the blacksmith's shed when he stoked his furnace too hot. There was talk that he had been making armor for the Roman Guard.

* * *

At the market, Rufus overhead a couple of merchants complaining that the gods Vulcan and Jupiter were at war with each other, that they were punishing Rome for its failures, and that Nero had interfered with their conflict, bringing judgment on the city. The god, Vulcan, had strong connections with fire and volcanoes, making this a plausible possibility.

Rufus didn't believe in the Roman gods. Rufus was raised in a Jewish home. His father followed Jesus, adopting the Christian sect when Rufus was a young boy. There was only one God, the Lord. How Jesus, the Christ, fit into that picture was a source of controversy among the Jews. It had led to heated discussions in his uncle's butcher shop, where his father would often mill around discussing theology with other men. The two brothers, Rufus's father and his uncle, had forged a deep bond in their faith. So, to embrace the Vulcan scenario as an explanation seemed foolish to Rufus.

With the speed of a steed, the fire spread throughout Rome.

A windy night, the flames tore along the length of the Circus. The fire expanded through an area of narrow, twisting streets and packed apartment blocks. There were no stone buildings, temples, or large open areas of ground in these sections of the city that could impede the inferno. The Circus itself was a stone and brick edifice, but all the stables and outbuildings were wooden structures that become voracious fuel for the blaze's spread.

Rufus was in bed when his uncle stirred him. They fled the city, returning a couple of days later when the house and butcher shop were clear of danger.

The fire moved along the Palatine and Caelian

slopes. Rufus and his uncle could see the orange glow in the distance as they fled. Streets filled with people fleeing the flames, some escaping to areas unaffected by the fire while others to the open fields and rural roads outside the city.

Among crowds of refugees, many stories surfaced of looters and arsonists spreading the flames by throwing torches or acting in groups, hindering counter measures that were being made to halt or slow the progress of the flames. Groups responsible for throwing torches and stopping those from fighting the fire claimed they were under orders to do so. Rufus's uncle asked about this, but no one substantiated the rumors. The claims confused Rufus. Why would someone create more fires? Who would prevent others from putting it out?

The fire appeared to stop after six or seven days of continuous burning, but it flared up again and smoldered for yet another week. Some folks they talked with in the fields outside the city described huge flames engulfing buildings with such haste that no one could stop it. The edifices in Rome were situated very near each other, making them vulnerable to the fire's uncontrollable spread.

While people, scrambling from the fire, moved out of the city, looters took advantage of the situation — robbing people, homes, and buildings. Some people stayed in their neighborhoods at significant risk, trying to prevent damage or loss.

The fire destroyed three of Rome's fourteen

districts and damaged an additional seven. Rufus's home was in one area that was not affected by the flames. The general direction of the inferno's progress drew close to their district, but the winds shifted it north before it reached them.

Afterward, when officials assessed the damage, it was apparent that most of Rome's quarter of a million inhabitants fled the city. The fire killed about 12,000 people and destroyed over 14,000 buildings. It was impossible to determine the number of animals lost, or the property stolen or destroyed.

Many who believed the various prophecies that fire would destroy Rome were wondering if these prophecies were coming true now.

Rufus's uncle lamented the difficulty this would be for Rome. "There will be hard days ahead."

Scuttlebutt suggested that Nero was in a nearby tower during the blaze. Anecdotes claimed he dressed himself up in theater garb, make-up and all.

There were other reports that Nero was away from Rome when it broke out. "Nero was in a nearby village," someone said. Others rumored Nero had returned to the city and was taking measures to bring in food supplies and to open gardens and public buildings to accommodate refugees and help the citizenry. With so much hearsay, it was difficult to know what was true.

Back at the butcher shop, Rufus and his uncle heard the gossip that circulated. The shop was busier than normal because of the destruction and the displacement of people from other districts. Supplies were low, and Uncle Ephron worried they would not have enough meat. Butchers sold a wide variety of meat — pork, beef, goat, wild boar, rabbit, and geese. Much of this wouldn't be available in the coming months.

The store's patrons talked about the fervor in Rome. Because of the quirky rumors, additional gossip circulated that the emperor himself had started the fire. People would place orders while chatting about the latest story.

"Motivated by his desire to destroy the city," one customer asserted, "Nero, unbeknownst to his aides, sent out men pretending to be drunk to set fire to the city. He watched the fire from his palace singing and playing his lyre."

"Nero destroyed the city so he could rebuild Rome the way he wanted," another said.

"I understand Nero started the fire to blame someone else for it," an elderly gentleman claimed as he picked up his lamb chops. "He's blaming the already unpopular Christians."

Rufus and his uncle glanced at each other.

BURNING
QUESTIONS

The four of them stood together off the square — Rufus, Agnus, Polonius, and Joshua. The brief break from his labor at the butcher shop relieved Rufus. He often joined his young peers, who also had respite from their work to catch up on the latest rumors and plan their activities for the approaching sabbath.

The hushed intensity of the moment replaced the usual playful chatter.

"Yesterday was awful," said Agnus. "I'm still looking over my shoulder when I walk in the streets."

Pushed back across her forehead, Agnus' auburn hair was striking as it peeked from its scarf. She was referring to their confrontation with the soldiers. Polonius was there on the other side of the market. Joshua had heard about it. Word had passed with staccato across the district. Everyone knew.

"My heart's still beating fast." Polonius patted his hand against his chest several times. "When I saw you both crushed by the soldiers, all I could do was panic. Do you think the officials believe that we're a church?" Polonius scrunched his face; his peach fuzz beard glistened in the sunshine.

"It's hard to say," Rufus answered, and then quietly he said, "We've all been careful, but of course, you understand that as followers of Jesus, we are different."

"Followers of Jesus," Joshua echoed his friend with a whisper.

"Didn't he ask if you were a Jew?" Polonius asked. "Why did he ask that?"

"Do you think they've seen you at one of our gatherings?" Joshua asked. "Why else would they ask that?"

Agnus stepped into the middle of them and waved her hands.

"We shouldn't be talking out here," she said. "Someone might be listening to us."

Agnus was always the most cautious of the quartet. The young men were constantly developing crazy schemes. Agnus often reeled them in. Being Jewish was hard enough in Rome; following Jesus was even more difficult.

Joshua spoke with his hand covering his mouth. "I'm just scared that these rumors I've overheard might be true."

Agnus looked over her shoulder at a couple walking past them. From their appearance, they were Roman citizens. Their prominent foreheads scanned the plaza as they walked across it.

"It's hard enough," Joshua muttered.

Whatever responsibility Nero bore for the disaster, the rumors were true. Nero had begun a scheme to deflect any attention from himself by faulting members of the fledgling Christian religion for the blaze.

"Well," Joshua said, "everyone says that Caesar has ordered the rundown of Christians. He's blaming us for the fire."

"You understand what that means." Angus looked at Rufus.

Rufus's father had been the victim of one of Caesar's tirades.

In the past, Caesar and his governors had used many creative and brutal persecutions to punish those who offended the empire. Because of their allegiance to God, whom they called King, Christians often found themselves in the crosshairs of the government. Officials condemned some to be dressed in animal skins and torn apart by dogs, while they burned others to death in nighttime pyres that provided light for the emperor's garden parties.

Soldiers had rounded Rufus's father up a few years back. He never returned, and no one knew what happened to him. For over a year, Rufus and his uncle used every spare moment to scour Rome for any information about him. Rufus could only hope that they had consigned him to be a galley slave in one of the navy's war vessels. At least he would still be alive.

"Yes, I guess I do." Rufus looked down at the ground. He kicked his sandal at the cobblestone. He missed his father something terrible.

Angus snuck her hand down by her side and reached to grab Rufus's clenched fist.

Polonius let out a gust of air. The others responded to the sound by looking at him.

"I get following Jesus is hard." He shrugged. "Sometimes I'm just not convinced. I have doubts, if you get what I mean. And then when it gets hard, well, I'm just not sure."

"Yes," Joshua said, "but you shouldn't doubt."

"Maybe I shouldn't; but I do."

Agnus reached out her other arm and grabbed Polonius behind the elbow. She gave him a gentle squeeze. He glanced at her.

"What if they come back? What if they find out we're a church?"

They all looked at Polonius.

"We could end up like your father, Rufus."

Rufus stared back at his feet. Familiar pains crept up into his chest as his simmering emotions felt suffocating.

"We should get back to work." Again, Agnus

displayed her wisdom. "Our God remains king of all. You understand that."

The four of them gave each other brisk kisses and hugs and broke their circle. Rufus stood there, looking around the square. He saw Agnus, her thick, long hair leaking through her scarf. He smiled, watching her as she approached her mother's cart across the plaza. Agnus's little sister was sitting in the doorway of a small gray tent pitched alongside of it.

Rufus watched as Agnus greeted the old man selling flowers, spices, and various pots next to her mother. The hunched gentleman smiled as he handed Agnus a sprig of lavender, which she brought to her nose and enjoyed. Rufus smiled too, and he turned back to the shop.

A couple of blocks from the square, Uncle Ephron's butcher shop was always a place of comfort. Despite the violent and bloody work, a peaceful warmth hovered over the place. The momentary turbulence in Rufus's mind longed for the comfort of that space. He hastened his steps as he turned the corner toward the store.

BUTCHER'S SHOP

Rufus returned to his uncle's shop. He snatched up his apron and a broom and got back to his afternoon routine. Cleaning up after the morning slaughter was always mindless work. It provided space for Rufus to process the world around him. He breathed in and out as he swept. It calmed him.

Today, it felt necessary. His thoughts were a disheveled mess. Angst about the fire and the turn of events in Rome, thoughts about his father, concern with the doubts that Polonius had expressed in his mind. Though he hated to admit it, sometimes he had doubts, too.

He leaned against the broom and recalled John Mark's warning from the scroll of Isaiah: "young men shall fall exhausted." His brain felt tired. The flurry of the last couple of weeks was taking a toll on him.

What was Mark's antidote for weariness? "Think," Rufus spoke out loud to only himself.

Yes, he remembered, the ones who wait for the Lord will have their strength renewed. And then his favorite part: they will mount up with wings like eagles; they will run and not be weary; they will walk and not faint.

But how? What did it mean to wait on the Lord?

"Are you just standing there?" His uncle had entered the back of the shop. "Last I checked that broom can't push itself."

"Oh, I know that," Rufus replied. "I was just thinking."

"Yes, and what might you be thinking about?"

"Do you remember when John Mark read from Isaiah a couple of weeks ago, the part about the eagles?"

Rufus looked at his uncle — the blood stains on his apron, the streaks of gray through his smokey-black hair, the lines of concern across his forehead. Rufus loved no one more since his father had vanished.

"Ah yes, the scrolls of Isaiah. There is much there to reflect about. However, young man, the broom still will not move itself. Let's get our work done, and then we can discuss the prophets."

Rufus got back to his sweeping, still reflecting on John Mark and the book of Isaiah. Mark often quoted from the prophets, and Rufus loved listening to Mark recite passages from Isaiah. He never asked, but he was sure it was Mark's favorite scroll.

Later that afternoon, Mark visited the butcher shop with some others from the synagogue. They stood around the counter and deliberated with Uncle Ephron. Rufus was packing meat from the drying rack near the back. He listened in on the discussion.

"We are in, what I would call, the second Exodus." Mark spoke with a tender expression. "It is the better and final Exodus."

"I'm not sure I get your point," the man standing next to Mark said.

"In the days of Moses, Israel's defining moment was when the Lord glorified himself, redeemed Israel from bondage, destroyed her enemies, made a covenant with her, and led her to the Promised Land. Would you agree with that?"

The men all nodded.

"I imagine Isaiah rehearsed that exodus story, but with an eye to the future when he wrote, 'Prepare the way of the Lord; make straight his path.' While he was recalling the past, he was expecting a future exodus led by the Messiah himself. Messiah would lead God's people from bondage, not only from tyranny, but from Satan and sin's rule in their lives."

"I would agree," Rufus's uncle said, "but how is it you speak of it as a second Exodus?"

"Perhaps more than any other scroll," Mark said to the men, "Isaiah portrays Israel's restoration through the Lord's promises. Yahweh guarantees to manifest his glory and repeat the mountaintop experience at

Sinai. Like the first Exodus, he will lead Israel through water. The Scriptures say, 'When you pass through the waters, I will be with you; and when you pass through the rivers, they will not sweep over you.'"

The men bowed their heads out of respect for the prophet Isaiah. Together in unison, they called out, "To the prophet Isaiah."

Mark continued. "He promised to guide Israel through the wilderness, as he did in a cloud. 'The Lord will go before you. He will be your rear guard.' The Lord provided sustenance in the first Exodus, also in the second: 'They will feed beside the roads and find pasture on every barren hill. They will neither hunger nor thirst, nor will the desert heat or the sun beat down on them. He who has compassion on them will guide them and lead them beside springs of water.'"

"To the prophet Isaiah."

"There is the prominent servant of Isaiah who will deliver God's people from their captivity in Babylon. Look rigorously; you can see these promises. They find satisfaction in Messiah, in Jesus. He is the new Moses, the greater Moses. Don't you see this?"

Mark paused. The men murmured to one another.

Like a saw zipping back and forth, cutting a piece of wood, one man shook his head from side to side in disbelief. "They crucified this Jesus you talk about. Everyone knows that. He couldn't be the Messiah."

"You are right; they crucified him." Mark acknowledged the objection. "There is one significant contrast between the first and the second Exodus: the writings of Moses, the prophets and the poets expect the second Exodus to be a consummate event. In the end, the Lord will deal with sin with great decisiveness. He will establish a faithful remnant. He will create a new heaven and a new earth. These events take place as God executes and completes the second Exodus. Would you agree?"

The objector nodded. The other men did as well.

"It was necessary," John said, "for the Messiah to die to deal with sin. The prophet understood this. 'He has born our griefs and carried our sorrows; yet we esteemed him stricken, smitten by God, and afflicted. But he was pierced for our transgressions; he was crushed for our iniquities; upon him was the chastisement that brought us peace, and with his wounds, we are healed. All we, like sheep, have gone astray; each has turned to his own way; and the Lord has laid on him the iniquity of us all.'"

"To the prophet Isaiah," they chanted, but then the arguments began.

Rufus finished the packaging and grabbed the broom again. Pushing the scraps on the floor with the broom into the dustpan, he dumped it into the refuse bin. Rufus loved it when the men came to the butcher shop to discuss theology. He always enjoyed listening. Mark was his favorite.

Mark introduced his final thoughts. "Isaiah's framework for a second Exodus points to Jesus. This coordinates with Isaiah's expectations of a brand-new day. I believe Jesus is Israel's God incarnate."

The men were from the synagogue. They were not from the gathering. At these words, they bristled. A new round of debate ricocheted throughout the shop as if the cattle had come back to life and were stampeding. It grew thunderous and heated. Mark's ideas had that effect on those who didn't believe in Messiah, Jesus.

Mark hushed the men.

"I must go, but I leave you with these thoughts. Jesus delivers Israel from its captivity, an enslavement marked by spiritual rather than physical bondage, a captivity by sin and pride. As a mighty warrior cloaked in a servant's garb, Jesus crushes Israel's true enemy — Satan. He leads his people through the wilderness, drives out their enemies from the Promised Land, defeating Satan and casting out his demonic forces. Once and for all, he establishes the promised end-time Kingdom. The Lord's glory now lives in the person of Jesus, who dwells with his people. He does this by taking on the role of Isaiah's suffering servant. Jesus suffers on behalf of the Israelites; he bears their curse. Think about it, but I must go."

The arguments resumed as Mark gathered his leather satchel. He left the group quarreling amongst themselves and moved to the door.

These common discussions exposed Rufus to

Mark's ideas. It still swept over him with wonder as he contemplated Mark's picture of Jesus, one who is Israel's sovereign Lord and Israel's suffering servant.

"He is Lord and servant," Rufus said to himself. He hung the broom and dustpan on the wall behind the door.

Mark had paused for a moment as he opened the shop's massive door, and Rufus took the opportunity to grab his attention.

"Sir, may I ask you a question before you go?"

"Only one," Mark answered. "I must get on my way."

"Sir, my friends and I are very concerned. We have doubts. With the new suffering, well, it's just hard."

"Ah, yes, young Rufus, I understand your concern. To follow the Messiah is a hard path. I had doubts when I was young. Persevere in your faith, Rufus; the Lord will show himself to you."

Somehow, hoping for something more, Rufus lowered his head to the broom's bristles.

Mark sensed Rufus's disappointment and leaned over.

"Ah, I remember what my mentor, Peter, would say to those who trusted Jesus. 'Though you have not seen him, you love him. Though you don't see him, you believe in him. You rejoice with a joy that is inexpressible and filled with glory. Bless your day, Rufus.'"

"Yours as well, sir." Rufus stared, watching the

heavy wooden door close behind the man.

JOHN MARK

John Mark was the cousin of Barnabas, who, as a force in the growing church throughout the world, had a reputation as an encourager.

Many conversations included mention of Barnabas. In discussions about the pioneers of the faith, conversation often could spin like a top to something negative. The men and women who led the charge lived rough-around-the-edges lives, and criticism could be blunt. When it was, someone disquieted by the negative would bring up a story about Barnabas.

His cousin — not so much. Many tagged John Mark as a quitter. He was "fragile." When the gathering at Rome met with him, reservation and hesitation swirled through the meeting. "What has this slight, fainthearted man to offer us?"

Mark deserted Paul and Barnabas in Pamphylia. He quit and left the mission behind. Mark admitted to the group of Roman Christians who interviewed him he had deserted his cousin and Paul at a crucial time. While in Cyprus, they experienced a fruitless time — there had only been one conversion, and they experienced strong demonic opposition to their work. Mark confessed it was a frightening stretch for his younger self, but he insisted he lived differently now. He described his discouragement at the hardness of the way and talked about his decision to return to the comforts of home. He spoke of his disappointment with himself and the dark days that followed.

"It was the Lord Jesus who rescued me from my despair," he said.

When Rufus first listened to Mark speak, he admitted that the man engaged him with his talk. Moderate in stature and somewhat handsome, his unkempt hair with its curls swirling every which way, he showed no eloquence. Neither his Greek nor his Aramaic matched literary standards, but what he said resonated with a magical profoundness. It excited Rufus.

Mark studied the Torah with diligent devotion. They salt-and-peppered his ideas. He saturated his conversations with phrases from the scrolls. He inspired listeners, believers, and non-believers alike.

In his initial interview in Rome, he told stories about his cousin Barnabas, the "son of encouragement." That endeared Rufus to Mark. Rufus's own uncle was central to his life. Rufus thought that his uncle, Ephron, too, provided solid support. His uncle often had a word to raise one's spirits. He was positive and gave Rufus amazing confidence.

John Mark's cousin, Barnabas, desired to forgive his failure and to give him another chance. Some in Jerusalem took the more serious view: missionary work requires dedication and endurance. They saw John Mark as a risk to the goal.

Many, through the years, had taken sides in the debate. Paul was right. No, Barnabas was right. Rufus's uncle, again the encourager, saw delight that the church sent two groups of missionaries out. Twice as many spread the gospel, twice as many places reached.

"God's work is wise," his uncle would say, "and without explanation."

Mark told the initial group of interviewers that he had sailed off to Cyprus with his cousin Barnabas. They had a successful journey, and Mark found it much better the second time around. That was not the end of his story. Years later, he would be back in the service of Paul, who would call him a "fellow worker." Rufus had a hunch that this was part of the wonderful working of God in the church.

He reflected on the time he was at the gathering when word came that the apostle Paul, imprisoned in Rome, asked his protégé Timothy to send for Mark because he would be helpful to him in his ministry. Rufus's uncle endorsed Mark, saying that he had matured through the years and was now a faithful servant of the Lord.

Even Paul, by then, recognized his progress and

considered him a valuable companion.

* * *

So, when Rufus saw John Mark in the shop today, his heart skipped with delight. It was always good when he visited.

Rufus was glad to hear that he would also be at the gathering that evening.

After work, Rufus made his way to Priscilla's shop, hoping to see Agnus. Her mother and father were tent makers. In their shop, they wove camel and goat hair into strips of cloth. Then they would sew the strips together to make tents for travelers. He often found Agnus at a loom, weaving the hairs together. He loved the smell of the space. Leather and wool. The tent maker would sew Roman tents from the leather hides of goats or cows. Of course, goats were many and less expensive than the hide of a cow. The rich in Rome would often order coverings or sun awnings for their private houses made from linen, which came from the city of Tarsus. The tent makers would sew these structures as well.

Rufus entered the store. Aquila greeted him. "Good afternoon, young Rufus. How is your uncle?" "He is fine, Mr. Tentmaker."

"Young Rufus," was the old tent maker's nickname for him. Rufus would always play back with the ominous "Mr. Tentmaker" title.

"I doubt you're here to visit me," Aquila said. He rubbed his worn hands on his apron to clean them some. He reached out and gave the young man a hug. It was a bear hug — the kind that hurts and provides massive comfort all at once.

"Agnus will be back any time. Sit. Sit. She went to the goat herder's farm for supplies."

Rufus found a stool.

Aquila resumed stacking hides near the rear of the store. These materials would become tents and bags for sale; some would end up on Priscilla's cart in the forum market.

"Agnus and Priscilla told me about the incident yesterday," Aquila yelled from the back. "Are you alright? Were you hurt?"

"I'm fine. It was alarming, but it turned out all right. I worried about Agnus and then, when we came upon the stuck cart, I felt even more concerned."

"Thanks for helping. Priscilla sure appreciated it. I do too. You're so kind to us."

They talked for a while. Aquila explained about some of the new tents that different customers ordered from the tent maker. It became apparent after a bit that Agnus was late.

"I need to go, sir. My uncle is expecting me."

"Very well. I'm glad you stopped. Please wish your uncle well for me."

"Thank you. Tell Agnus I stopped. Are you going to

the gathering tonight?"

There were rumors that Mark had been laboring over something that would help the church in Rome grapple with the increasing heat that was rumbling throughout the city. With his endearment for the leader, Rufus was eager to receive what Mark developed for them. He wouldn't miss the meeting.

"We will be there if we can navigate without mischief."

"If my uncle doesn't need me, I'll walk with you."

"That would be nice, but you don't need to worry about us."

GATHERING

An hour later, Rufus's uncle sliced a slab of lamb for a customer. Nearing dusk, Rufus stacked the tools and knives away. He loved the end of the day. The climb up the stairs with his uncle to their home above the shop highlighted most evenings.

Just as his uncle swung the door closed, a child outside began yelling at him. He waved his arms. They were moving so fast he seemed an octopus.

"Bar Jonas, Bar Jonas. Phoebe asked me to give you a message. Please wait!"

The boy arrived at the portal. Without waiting to breathe, he bent over and scratched two lines in the dirt. Rufus recognized what the boy had drawn.

"The twelfth hour! At the twelfth hour!" The boy blurted in a gasp of a whisper.

With as much surprise, he disappeared.

Rufus's uncle used his sandals to scuff the lines into

nonexistence like the boy. He entered the shop and barred the door.

They climbed the stairwell in silence, but Rufus's inner world whirled. They already planned to be at the meeting. However, the urgency of the messenger boy unsettled them.

As they entered the upstairs apartment, his uncle said to him as soon as he shut the door, "The gathering meets tonight, as usual, but we will meet at a different time. You should accompany me rather than Agnus's family."

"I wouldn't miss it, my dear uncle. Agnus's father said they didn't need my help. And," Rufus paused, "Mark has been working on something special."

"Ah, I don't understand how you learn these things, boy."

Rufus knew that something had his uncle very concerned. He would only use the diminutive term of endearment when he was worried or bothered.

A couple of hours later, Rufus walked with his uncle at a brisk pace down the *Appian Way*. The sun slipped below the horizon but left a slight glow in the dusk. Just outside the city, his uncle turned off the road.

"Where are we going?" Rufus asked.

"What you may not have heard, Rufus," his uncle said, "is that the gathering changed locations. That was the urgent message the boy brought as we were closing."

If it had been lighter, Rufus would have recognized the tunnels and outbuildings of the city's burial grounds.

He had been there when his uncle had purchased space for burying his brother, Rufus's father. Of course, they never found him, and the tomb remained empty for years.

"It will serve our family well," his uncle would say when his wife asked him why he held onto the tomb. "We will keep it."

A couple of years later, Uncle Ephron buried his wife, Rufus's aunt, who passed away after a severe illness. He buried her there. That was another season that deepened the bond between the man and Rufus.

"What are we doing here?" Rufus asked his uncle as they neared a torch lit entrance to the catacombs.

"This is the new gathering place for now." His uncle nodded at a tall, young man who was just inside the opening.

The smell of myrrh and rosemary snuck through the air. Rufus followed his uncle around a couple of corners and into a crowded chamber. There were many familiar faces. Rufus saw Agnus and Priscilla. Agnus smiled when she saw him. He tilted his head in acknowledgment.

It was stifling and noisy. Someone had trimmed the lanterns low. They lined the sepulchers. The flickering shadows gave a peculiar feel to an already eerie place.

John Mark stood at the center of the assembly. The

murmur was loud. His hair was shorter and graying, but still curly. He was aging well. His beard, also gray, distinguished him. His chestnut skin wrinkled with grace at the corner of his brunette eyes.

He held in his hand a scroll. The clean ivory color and crisp edges of the papyrus betrayed its newness. It didn't have the traditional olive wood handles of the scrolls at the synagogue.

Rufus had studied the scrolls at the synagogue. He learned they were many sheets of papyrus glued in a long succession, with two different sides — one with fibers running across the papyrus, the other with fibers running vertical. The interior of the scroll was known as the *recto*.

Rufus looked at the *verso*, the outside of the parchment, as Mark held it in front of the group gathered. He observed the vertical fibers of the papyrus making up the outside. The vertical fibers flexed, pulling apart when the reader rolled them up. This structure made it is easier to wind the scroll and allowed for greater durability.

Gluing these pieces together with glue purchased from a butcher shop was the work of artisans. Occasionally, Rufus's uncle would mix up glue for a customer. Rufus hated the way it stank when he made it. It burned his nostrils and gave him a headache. He was glad his uncle didn't do it often, and that they lived in a lesser part of town where making papyrus was rare.

Mark raised the scroll above his head and waved it. The crowd stilled.

"Let's pray," he said. "Father God, you are here. Fill us with your Spirit. Protect us and give us radical boldness. Amen."

There was an attentive chorus of "amens" throughout. The group sang several hymns. They broke bread together and took wine, remembering Jesus. The elders prayed for several individuals in the assembly. Then, they invited Mark to speak.

"These are troubling times." His voice was robust, holding tones of tempered passion and zeal. "The persecution is intensifying. We are under siege. Some of our brothers and sisters have gone to be with our King." Mark paused, took a deep breath, and sighed. "Some of you have lost your homes in the fire, others have lost jobs."

With this, the crowd stirred again.

"That's right," answered a concerned listener.

"What am I going to do?" came a troubled question.

"I'm in a horrible spot. I don't know what to do either." Someone huffed out of desperation.

More expressions of angst reverberated throughout the grotto.

He waved the parchment again. The murmuring calmed.

"In these troubling times and with difficulties ahead, we need to find encouragement in our bond with Jesus, the Christ. I have spent the last several months writing out the stories that Peter recounted to me during my times with him. His stories about Jesus will be an encouragement to you, and I have come tonight to read them. They could prove helpful in the certain hardships that we will be facing."

Again, the crowd stirred. Rufus could see several people talking amongst themselves. A woman beside his uncle Ephron broke out in sobs. It grew louder and louder. Rufus struggled to breathe as the room warmed. The odor of burning oil was overtaking the spicy aromas from the tombs.

The din increased until a man yelled. His words were indiscernible, but loud enough that the noise tapered.

"Phoebe wants to speak."

Rufus knew the elderly lady well. He strained to see her; he wasn't quite tall enough, and she was short. She had been a customer at the shop for many years. Her gray hair was always pulled back in a tight bun, which caused the distinguished features of her face to stand out. Her darksome skin was smooth, making one wonder how old she might be.

"These are indeed troubling times for us, John Mark." She spoke straight at him, but all could overhear her. "It would be meaningful for you to read what you have written." She nodded. "Please, read them to us."

"It's getting late," a man from the back said.

"It is, and we risk being discovered. However, these crypts will provide ample cover, and the people seem willing to listen. I think it will be all right." She turned to Mark. Several elders nodded in agreement.

"If you need to go, now is a good time. Those who wish to stay and hear Mark's thoughts, please stay. Again, this is crucial. For those who are leaving, may I remind you to stagger your exit? We must continue to do everything we can to stay out of the soldiers' notice."

Turning to Mark, she said, "Mark, I sense an urgency in our situation. Even should the Lord tarry, these are the last days. In these days, there is no 'later.'"

"Wonderful," Mark said, and he unrolled his scroll.

THE SCROLL

From his seat on the floor, Rufus could see the lamp's glow shine through the scroll. He saw the shadow of Mark's writing, the fine Greek penmanship. He noticed the first seam where the glue held the pieces of the scroll together. Rufus leaned forward.

The crowd shifted around him, many attempting to seat themselves or squat against a nearby wall. Several people had left. No one questioned them. Rufus sat beside his uncle, anticipating Mark's words.

The noise quelled. With a grip on the scroll before him, Mark read. With deep projection and tender, tenor tones, Mark began.

"The beginning of the gospel of Jesus Christ, the Son of God."

He paused, allowing the timbre of his voice to bounce off the chamber's stone and mud walls. Rufus recalled the words from the scroll of Moses, "In the beginning, God created."

Mark resumed.

"As Isaiah the prophet wrote, 'Behold, I send my messenger before your face, who will prepare your way, the voice of one crying in the wilderness: Prepare the way of the Lord, make his paths straight.'"

Rufus recognized the words from the prophet combined with those of another prophet — Malachi, perhaps. He couldn't remember. Rufus knew Israel had waited a long, long time for its Messiah.

Rufus's early synagogue school emphasized a coming Messiah. The rabbis had encouraged him to memorize and meditate on substantial portions of Scriptures. His young, agile mind picked it up like rare fruits or nuts. Its taste intrigued him, and he wanted more.

It often surprised Rufus when, years later, he would recall a passage he had learned. It was easy to identify Isaiah or Moses when he heard them; Malachi, not so much, although they all rang out with the same message — creation, commission, rebellion, and redemption.

Mark read on.

"John appeared, baptizing in the wilderness and proclaiming a baptism of repentance for the forgiveness of sins."

"Ah, John, the Baptist," Rufus reflected.

His father used to tell him stories of John the Baptist. In fact, as a boy, Rufus was positive his father was just like John. The child of a butcher, Rufus's father, had grown up herding animals, wearing their skins, and eating crazy foods in the fields while caring for the family's flock. The adventure stories he told Rufus were abundant fodder for his boyish imagination. He dreamed of remote areas with untamed beasts, fields with wild berries and bugs, and places of pulsating vividness.

And like John the Baptist, Rufus's father spoke often about Jesus and his Kingdom. These conversations remained with Rufus from the earliest memories of his parents — stories and Jesus.

Rufus returned his attention to the storyteller as he recounted Jesus' baptism by John. Mark referred to a voice from heaven, declaring pleasure with Jesus.

"And a voice came from heaven, 'You are my beloved Son; with you I am well pleased.'"

Did Peter, Mark's source for these stories, hear the voice from heaven? Rufus wondered what it sounded like. Was it tender? Did the voice boom loud? Did everyone pay attention? What was the look on Jesus' face? Calm? Did he smile like Rufus might when his uncle complimented him on his work? Or did seriousness consume Jesus?

Next, Mark recited the strange story about Jesus' temptation in the wilderness.

"Wilderness," Rufus thought, "is a laboratory for Israel." His boyhood rabbi had repeated that phrase again and again. In the Exodus from Egypt, God tested Israel, and she failed. The testing cost them forty years of wilderness wandering.

It seemed obvious to Rufus, because of hearing Mark talk in the shop, that Mark's initial use of the Isaiah quote was a signpost beckoning the listeners to remember Isaiah's broad message of return from exile and redemption by the messianic servant figure.

Rufus was aware from his studies that the last third of Isaiah's scroll was a retelling of the exodus story. It was clearer now that John the Baptist's role heralded Isaiah's new exodus, exactly the way Mark was saying earlier that day.

"But a renewed exodus from what?" Rufus posed the question to himself.

He visualized Mark's delicate contrast. Israel had failed in the exodus of Moses. Mark was comparing their failure with something new in Jesus. Israel had sinned in the wilderness. Not so for Jesus. He was in the harsh, desolate place with animals for forty days without faltering.

"Who could do that?" Rufus thought.

There was a common Roman genre known as "a life." Developed in Greek culture and improved by Romans, this style of biography was a story. In it, the author would incorporate a variety of literary styles to tell the heroic narrative of a figure — a hero worthy of the audience's attention. "The life" might include history, praise, or moral philosophy. It invoked the listener's confidence in this individual, the same conviction that the author held.

As Mark read his opening, "the life" swept Rufus away. Mark invited him to engage Jesus in a new way.

"Who could do that?" Rufus thought of the man as Mark read of wild beasts and angels. "Who?"

THE READING

Rufus watched Mark; he had paused. A woman nearby held out a jug to him. Releasing the scroll to her, he pulled it toward himself, turned away from the audience, and took a drink. He handed the vessel back to the lady and lifted the parchment, rolling to the next section.

"Now, after John was arrested, Jesus came into Galilee, proclaiming the gospel of God, and saying, 'The time is fulfilled, and the Kingdom of God is at hand; repent and believe in the gospel.'"

These words felt familiar. His uncle or Mark would say this to the men who gathered in the butcher shop — repent and believe. His father, also, had spoken often about the Kingdom of God before his disappearance. It heartened Rufus, though he still found himself unsettled as to its meaning.

Mark cleared his throat and read what he had written about the summoning of the disciples. Jesus calls Peter, Andrew, James, and John to follow him at the outset of his ministry in Galilee. "Follow me." Mark repeated it several times. "And Jesus said to them, 'Follow me, and I will make you become fishers of men.'" Could these men be the fishers of Jeremiah's prophecy calling the remnant of God's people back?

"What must it have been like," Rufus thought to himself, "to be those men and to leave those boats on that shore?" It was not a new thought by any means. What does it take to follow Messiah? What would it be like to leave the security and safety of his uncle's shop behind? Something inside Rufus wanted to find out — to experience the-wind-blowing-through-your-hair adventure of it.

In a flash, he thought of his absent father. Fear returned. The strain between longing and fear made the hair on his arms stand at attention.

Who was this Jesus that called people to follow him? No prophet before had called others to follow himself. Instead, prophets would charge people to follow the Lord God. Was Jesus therefore making a tacit acknowledgement that he had divine authority by commanding others to follow him. Who was this man?

Rufus had often heard John Mark speak about the need to follow Jesus as Messiah. "He is Christ to Jews and Romans alike," he would say. According to Mark, the unequivocal answer for everything involved loyal disciples sacrificing their lives and ambitions for the sake of the Messiah's kingdom.

Mark continued to read. Story after story about Jesus amassed before the onlookers. Mark must have said "immediately" twenty times. Rufus was out of breath, listening to the fast-paced narrative. He longed to stop at each account and ask questions or meditate on it.

Rufus imagined Mark reclining across the table from Peter, his "mentor" as he called him, gnawing dried fish or figs, and listening to stories about Jesus. Now he had woven these anecdotes together in this scroll with such deliberate purpose, and he was reading this collection for the gathering's encouragement and edification.

The arpeggio of amazing stories continued. Jesus heals the man with an unclean spirit. Many bring the sick to him. Jesus heals them. He heals a leper.

Jesus restores a fellow with a withered hand.

Men cut a hole in the roof and lower their friend through it. Jesus heals him, and get this, he forgives him.

Who does that?

Jesus claims to be the Lord of the Sabbath.

What did that mean? Rufus had grown up honoring the holy day. He learned by heart that God established the Sabbath in creation. The commandments from God that Moses gave the people codified it — keep the Sabbath holy. The rules and regulations he had learned in his childhood made it interesting.

Several of his Jewish friends had it difficult, having

to keep the rules. Rufus's father, and now his uncle, were soft on the strict guidelines, having become followers of Jesus. Though they often celebrated Sabbath, they put more emphasis on the first day of the week, calling it the Lord's Day.

For Polonius, the concept meant nothing. His Roman parents followed Jesus and not so much Moses. With Greek roots, Polonius didn't have any Jewish background apart from what his friends taught him. He saw Jesus differently but experienced him the same.

The rabbinical teachings prescribed how to live your life down the smallest detail — what to eat, what to drink, and the significance of every day on the calendar. What Rufus realized is that all those things were pointing to Jesus fulfilling of the Law. Polonius was less concerned with the law but more in awe of the massive authority Jesus had. Authority was important to the Greeks. So, he became a believer.

There was a friction rising as Mark spoke of the religious leaders and their conversations with Jesus. It was clear to Rufus as he listened; the issue was one of authority. He wondered what his friend Polonius was thinking as he listened.

Jesus preaches to enormous crowds.

He preaches to small clusters.

Jesus casts out demons.

He feeds five thousand people with next to nothing. There were twelve lunch pails leftover.

He heals a man by casting out a demon — a demon who cried out, naming Jesus the "Son of God."

Funny, Mark made no comment about this incident. He immediately moved on to the next story — Jesus being called crazy by his family.

Jesus feeds four thousand people with basketfuls left over.

Amazing, astonishing, remarkable. The people reacted to Mark's stories.

Mark would intersperse the episodes of wondrous events with brief snippets of Jesus' teaching. He spoke of fasting, of bridegrooms, of blaspheming the Holy Spirit. He told stories. Jesus spoke of a man sowing seeds. This was familiar to Rufus. His father had told him that story many times.

Jesus preaches about mustard seeds, lamps with baskets covering them, and ripened grain.

He calms a storm.

He walks on water.

Who does that?

Jesus discusses man's traditions, God's commandments, and the defiling of the human body.

Mark kept coming back to stories, highlighting the chafing between Jesus and the authorities. It mounted over their misunderstandings, their mistrust, and their jealousy of Jesus' impact.

Even the ones he had called to follow him seemed at a loss to understand him. Jesus explained everything to them. The tensity was speeding up in Mark's recounting of Jesus' life. Rufus could sense, brick-by-brick, the structure building. His pulse intensified as Mark told the stories about Jairus, the leader of a synagogue, and his daughter, plus the sickly woman. Rufus noticed a rip inside himself as Mark intertwined these two stories. He grimaced.

It had not been uncommon for Rufus to wander away from his uncle's cart at the *agora*, the market in the district square. He would sometimes mill over to the steps in front of the colonnades, where he would often find a band of artists performing. While most of it was in Latin, which Rufus knew, his favorites were the Greek poets and storytellers.

Rufus had grown skillful in his discernment of the structure of Greek and Hebrew literature. He loved listening for the climactic moment. It was repeatedly at the center of a poet's piece. If he caught it, as the orator intended, it would be the linchpin by which he could interpret the rest of the story or poem.

He became adept at watching and listening for this. One artist who often appeared at the market would say, "I see that sparkle in your eye, young man, when you get the gist." Rufus enjoyed the compliment.

Now, as he listened to Mark read from the scroll, Rufus was trying to watch for this type of apex. The building sensations gave him the impression that Mark was employing this same style in his writing.

Rufus empathized when Mark told of Jesus'

interaction with Jairus. His daughter was dying. Rufus understood the loss of a loved one, the pain, the disappointment, and the grief that would come to this man if she died.

At the same time, Rufus had grown up holding religious officials with skepticism. His father suspected many from Jerusalem to be corrupt, taking advantage of their positions. They hated Jesus. They hated those who spoke of him in the synagogue or the marketplace.

So, with surprise, Rufus reacted when Mark interrupted the story with another — of a woman in the crowd that slowed Jesus' progress to Jairus's house to heal the child. This put the little one at risk. Rufus didn't remember this story. And then, when Jesus stopped to talk with her while the man's daughter lay dying, Rufus grappled with offense. After all, who does that?

From the murmur in the room, Rufus became aware the story had unsettled others. Could it be Jesus' lack of urgency? Was it the dismissal of the ranking official for a woman in need? Was it the lowly nature of the woman or the prominent position of the official?

For Rufus, a new question emerged: "Who was on the inside and who was on the outside?" Something was unsettling as he thought about it. He tried to sort it out in his mind.

There was something amazing about this man, and

it scared Rufus.

A climax was developing. Rufus knew it the moment that Mark read the story of the blind man. And why did it take Jesus two attempts to make him see? What did that mean? And then, he heard Mark say that Jesus asked his disciples, "Do you not yet understand?"

Right in front of him, the buildup materialized. Nobody understood this amazing Jesus. Nobody on the inside, nobody on the outside. Jesus astounded the crowd, but none understood.

Mark highlighted Jesus, who asks the blind man, "Do you see anything?"

The blind man looked up and said, "I see people, but they look like trees, walking."

Mark finished the story this way: "Then Jesus laid his hands on his eyes again; and he opened his eyes. He restored his sight, and he saw everything clearly."

Rufus saw it. He didn't quite understand it, but he saw it.

The pinnacle was here. Mark read further.

"And Jesus went on with his disciples to the villages of Caesarea Philippi. And on the way he asked his disciples, 'Who do people say that I am?' And they told him, 'John the Baptist; and others say, Elijah; and others, one of the prophets.' And he asked them, 'But who do you say that I am?' Peter answered him, 'You are the Christ.' And he strictly charged them to tell no one about him."

An eerie hush, like the eye of a hurricane, passed through the cavern.

"That was it," Rufus thought to himself, "the moment, the climax, the apogee." Mark wanted them to ask, "Who do you say that I am?" Every comment, story, and idea about this amazing man drove his listeners to this question. "Who is he? Why are we so amazed by him? What is it about him?"

Who do you say that I am?

As John Mark took another drink, Rufus couldn't stop his thoughts from migrating in different directions. One thought, however, trapped his attention. Why? Why did Jesus say to his disciples, "Tell no one about me?" If he was the Messiah, this was a strange request; wasn't it?

If Jesus is the Christ, Rufus thought, it would have been natural to have massive expectations: the Messiah's reign and his kingdom are in the Christ of Malachi and in the Christ of Isaiah. Wasn't this the message of Daniel? The message of the prophets? From fall to redemption, this was worth celebrating with a blast of ram's horns or a clash of cymbals.

Yet, the hush remained hovering over the tombs.

AGNUS'S MOTHER AND FATHER

The pause was long. An elder clearing his throat broke the stillness of the catacombs.

Mark lowered the scroll and gave the man his attention. The bearded fellow rose to his feet and approached Mark.

"Mark, these are encouraging stories indeed. Our Savior is tremendous beyond words. We should end our gathering now and reconvene tomorrow to hear the rest of what you've written."

Mark nodded in agreement. The elder closed the assembly in prayer, asking that God would use Mark's words to stimulate growth and understanding in their hearers. Phoebe gave instructions to the crowd for disbursing. The group agreed to meet the following evening, an hour later, and in a different section of the grottoes.

Rufus found Agnus.

"What did you think?" he asked her.

"I love the stories of Jesus." Agnus looked at Rufus. "They make me wonder what it would be like if he came to our marketplace."

Rufus wasn't sure what to think. He wanted to hear more about what she thought.

Agnus and her parents left the catacombs along with Rufus and Ephron. They walked in silence. The bevy of sensations that filled Rufus were weighty. His thrill at Mark's presentation, the concern for the igniting persecution, and thoughts of Agnus all vied for his attention.

The moon was full and provided a pleasant light as they moved home. Rufus walked a step behind Agnus, and he watched her walk. He still wanted to hear more about what she was thinking after hearing Mark read. He assumed her opinions would be simple, thoughtful, heartfelt, and practical. His were gregarious, theological, and high-flying. They complemented each other well, he thought.

As they neared their district, the two groups split and headed for their homes. Rufus and his uncle climbed the narrow stairs to their apartment. Ephron allowed Rufus to go on for a bit about Mark's stories before yawning and encouraging him to rest. Rufus slept little; his thoughts were sprinting across his mind. He mulled over this mysterious Messiah and the tumultuous world around him.

✻ ✻ ✻

Two years prior, Uncle Ephron had invited Priscilla and Aquila to the apartment over the butcher shop for Sabbath Dinner. The prospect of hosting Agnus' parents excited Rufus, and his uncle assured him that Agnus would be there, too.

"I need you to make these deliveries," Rufus' uncle said, "and after you're done, fetch me some rosemary from the old man in the square."

He handed Rufus a pack of meat and a couple of coins and pushed him out the door.

"Hurry. The Sabbath never waits."

Rufus quickly made the deliveries and worked his way to the square, hoping he might bump into Agnus. He always savored those opportunities. It disappointed him when he arrived at the old man's cart to discover that Priscilla and her family had already closed and gone home.

As he took the sprigs of rosemary from the old man's hands, the merchant grabbed Rufus by the wrist and gazed at him.

"Fear not, young man, you will do much for the King's glory."

Startled, Rufus looked at the man and wondered what that could mean. He paid for his rosemary and returned to the shop, unnerved by the old man's comment.

"Finish down here for me," Ephron said. "I will see to the food. It is almost Sabbath."

Rufus did his usual wiping and sweeping. He stored the broom, latched the door to the shop, and walked upstairs to join his uncle. The aroma of roasted lamb and rosemary filled the apartment.

A short while later, the guests arrived and settled around the feast.

"It's finally Friday," his uncle said. He lit two candles and pushed them to the center of the rough, wood-hewn table. He closed his eyes and waved his hand in circles over the flames, as if scooping in some hope or joy.

"It is time to awaken our senses around the table. Before we eat, we set two candles out and as we light them, we invite the Sabbath to be in our home and surround us with the rest and joy of the Lord."

"Pray with me." He took a breath. "Blessed are You, Lord, our God, King of the Universe, who sanctifies us with his commandments, and bids us to light the candles of Sabbath. Amen."

"Amen," everyone responded in unison.

He offered similar blessings for the wine and the food.

Aquila cleared his throat and stood from his chair.

"Ephron, my friend," he spoke, "we should offer blessings for our children. I know we are no longer under the law, but the blessing of children is a marvelous tradition; don't you think?"

"I agree. Let's do so," Rufus's uncle replied.

With the smell of roast lamb begging to be eaten, the fathers invited their children to rise. They each laid their coarse, calloused hands upon Agnus's and Rufus's head.

"May God make you like Ephraim and Manasseh," Ephron recited from memory over Rufus.

And over Agnus, Aquila said, "May God make you like Sarah, Rebecca, Rachel, and Leah."

And then, in unison, they prayed. "May God Bless you and keep you. May his light shine upon you, and may he be gracious to you. May you feel God's Presence within you always, and may you find peace."

Rufus looked at Agnus.

She smiled.

He blushed.

The six of them settled into roast pork and lentils. The conversation between Ephron and Aquila was lively. At Ephron's request, Aquila described the days when they were in Corinth, where they had traveled to escape the Edict of Claudius.

Aquila rose again, and with a wave of his fork, acted the role of Claudius. "I, Tiberius Claudius Caesar Augustus Germanicus, Imperator, Pontifex Maximus, Holder of the Tribunal Power, Consul Designate, to the city of the Alexandrians, declare on this day, that since the Jews constantly make disturbances at the instigation of this Christ, I expel all of them from the city of Rome."

He waved his hand again, and they all laughed. Aquila was a formidable figure, with heavy shoulders and a captivating grin. He pulled his long brown hair back loosely into a ponytail as he sat down.

"We were not yet believers in the Messiah. In those days, questions about the identity of the Messiah divided the whole Jewish community in the city. Discussions about Jesus were new but disputed. The disputes became violent as the Jews sought to rid themselves of this offshoot. These clashes created problems for Rome. That's when the emperor made his edict, and we left."

"That must have been tough," Rufus said.

"It was hard, but not so much. We traveled to Corinth. It was a burgeoning city, and the tentmaker's trade was in great demand. We found much work and quickly. The place overwhelmed me, so we minded our own business and found a small synagogue to attend. Sometime later, we met Paul. He was looking for work and we had ample, so we hired him. It changed our life.

"Paul would go to the synagogue every Sabbath and try to persuade those there to follow Jesus. Eventually, the leaders rejected Paul's message, so he went into the marketplace and talked with Greeks and Gentiles.

"I must admit, I was very uncomfortable with this

at first. Our conversations in the shop were rather intense. We were back to division about who this man Jesus was. Having left Rome, the last thing we needed was to have trouble here. And yet, during those days, the Messiah opened our hearts to himself, and we became his followers. Life has never been the same.

"It was miraculous when Silas and Timothy arrived with finances from Macedonia, allowing Paul to preach full time. Those were incredible days. Eventually, Priscilla and I joined Paul when he left Corinth. We ended up with him in Ephesus, where we stayed and hosted a house church until we returned some years later to Rome."

Rufus sat there in awe. Each description fanned the embers of his desire to travel and see places. He knew about Corinth, a city of culture and wealth. It was famous for its temples and beaches. He knew less about Ephesus. He longed to see the world.

"I'm going to go to Ephesus someday," Rufus blurted out. By now, he had forgotten the old man's words.

Agnus looked at him.

He blushed again.

Agnus noticed and smiled.

MISSION EXPLAINED

Joshua and Polonius came by the butcher shop the next morning.

"What are you doing here?" Rufus asked. "Aren't you supposed to be working?"

Joshua's father did construction throughout the city. At sixteen, Joshua was learning the trade from his father. On a normal day, Joshua would accompany his father to the worksite and do odd jobs, occasionally being instructed on different aspects of the process. Today, his father left him at home concerned because of the rumored collecting of Christians. Joshua disliked his parents' zealousness for caution.

Polonius was the son of a jeweler. His father had learned the trade in Greece before moving to Rome, hoping to establish a thriving business. He had done well and was glad when his son showed interest in the trade. Now, the fires in Rome plummeted the demand for jewelry and there wasn't much work at the shop. So, when Joshua came by his father dismissed him with a warning to "be careful out there."

Uncle Ephron nodded to Rufus that he might take a break. The young men moved to the back of the shop. Rufus poured cups of water and passed around a loaf of bread.

"Well," Joshua spoke, "what did you think?"

They each understood what he was talking about.

"It was brilliant," Rufus answered. "I can't wait to hear the rest."

They also perceived that Rufus would have some uncanny insight into what John Mark had presented the night before. They settled in for some of his thoughts.

"So, Peter recognizes Jesus is the Messiah, right?"

"Right." Polonius said, and Joshua nodded in agreement.

"Joshua, you know that the Scriptures have traced these promises and their forthcoming fulfillment. The Messiah, descending from David, would bring about God's eternal Kingdom. He would destroy Israel's enemies. The promises were clear. But after years of silence, many wondered if someone would ever fulfill those promises."

"And suddenly, Peter blurts out that Jesus is the Messiah." Joshua tossed his half-eaten piece of bread into the air and caught it. "It must have been an eerie moment. What were they feeling, those men?"

He snatched a bite of the bread.

For an hour and a half, the young men discussed their impressions of God, Messiah, and John Mark. They rehearsed God's creation of the heavens and the earth. The world was to be his cosmic sanctuary, where he ruled and dwelled. Rufus and Joshua knew from the Scriptures that God designed all creation to house and display his glory.

It intrigued Polonius when Joshua said, "God created Adam and Eve as kings and commissioned them to rule on his behalf. He commissioned them to serve as priests, mediating his glory to the earth. God intended that humanity remain dependent on him, representing him on the earth."

"So," Polonius asked, "God gave them authority over his creation?"

"Yes," Rufus said, "that was his intention, but it didn't last long. Adam and Eve, desiring to be independent of God, succumbed to Satan's temptation, and it became a mess."

Rufus retold story after story of the devastation. It was clear the rebellion had left a calamitous blotch on God's creation, a blemish that rippled through the ages and continued to disrupt the young men's world. Polonius was an observant listener.

"Things haven't changed much; have they?"

"No, not at all," Rufus said. "I'm sure that's why God sent the prophets. They would assure God's people that despite this disastrous collapse and the subsequent debacles of Israel's faithlessness, God would overcome evil and establish a perfect dwelling place for his glory and Kingdom. He would restore it to its rightful splendor. And so, Israel waited and waited. They waited for a Messiah and for a king who would do just that."

"You sound more like Mark every day." Joshua reached over and gave Rufus a gentle push.

They laughed.

Rufus thought to himself, "This is the world that Jesus entered, and the world that I live in — a fallen mess. I'm a fallen mess, myself." He paused momentarily while sitting with his friends, and churned through these ideas, seeking a respite. Could Mark's scroll explain the pull between the rebellion and the promise? Could it connect with the hopes and longings of his people or of Rufus?

"Sometimes, I don't get it." Polonius interrupted Rufus's thoughts. "We're an obscure fellowship of people hiding away in a grotto in Rome, and Mark is telling us that John the Baptist entered this world, paving the way for Jesus, and pointing to him as the long-awaited fulfillment of promises made. It doesn't seem like much has changed. Do you know what I mean?"

It was quiet for a moment. Rufus had to admit that it was difficult to understand the persistent oppression suffered by God's people.

"Don't you suppose it seemed to confuse Jesus' disciples, too?"

It concerned these young men and those of Rufus's age, this era when Roman rule beat people down and sin persisted. These were questions for both the believers and the non-believing Jews who would talk in the butcher shop, despising the Roman interference with their faith.

As he sat there looking at his friends, Rufus increasingly knew that Mark had woven the stories of Jesus together so that they would be evermore certain of Jesus' identity and the nature of the Kingdom. Rufus convinced himself this was the new exodus of the butcher's store debates — an exodus from the effects of sin, an entrance to the forgiveness of sins, a pouring out of the Spirit, and the dawn of the new creation. He just had to wait to see it.

Who do you say that I am?

"Excuse me," Rufus's uncle interrupted. "We need to finish our work so we can go to the gathering tonight."

With that, the discussion finished, and Rufus's friend departed.

RECONVENED

Evening came quickly, and the gathering reassembled in a different recess of the catacombs. While the lanterns burned, they prayed together, and then they broke bread, as was customary each time they met. After singing, the elder invited Mark to finish his reading of the scroll.

"And he began to teach them," Mark read, "that the Son of Man must suffer many things and be rejected by the elders and the chief priests and the scribes and be killed, and after three days rise again."

Mark's audience reacted, sending a clamor through the entire room.

He continued. "And he said this plainly. And Peter took him aside and began to rebuke him."

Someone pitched in a hearty, "Yes."

John Mark looked up and then at the parchment, while behind him a man put oil into a lamp.

"But turning and seeing his disciples," Mark read,

"he rebuked Peter and said, 'Get behind me, Satan! For you are not setting your mind on the things of God, but on the things of man.'"

Another murmur swept through the crowd. Rufus sensed the tension, not only in the cave, but in himself as well. If Jesus had been Messiah, things should be better for them, shouldn't they? Instead, they met in hiding and fear. They ran from their Roman enemies. It troubled them.

Mark read on. Twice more, Jesus predicted the suffering he would endure. It remained unsettling to those listening. What point could Mark be making? Each time, Jesus invited his followers to join him in this way of life.

Was this — what they were experiencing now — the "way of life?" Here they were, Rufus, his uncle, and these people, under cover of darkness, listening to words about Messiah, while hiding in a cave. It made little sense, and their apprehensions persisted. They often discussed the promises of God, but when the heat pressed them, some doubted.

Was Jesus implying that suffering would mark his Kingdom, but not triumph? Did Peter and the other disciples experience this same intense discomfort that hung over this room? Mark painted a picture of those men, and it wasn't pretty. They were naïve and struggling to understand.

At the pinnacle of Mark's teaching, Peter acknowledges Jesus is the Christ, and then Jesus says he's going to die, and he tells them to hush about it. Who does that? If these promises were true and if Jesus was their fulfillment, why would he tell people to be quiet about him? Why not announce it to the world?

Time slowed as Rufus breathed in Mark's words. What was Mark saying with these stories? Rufus recollected passages from the prophets, hinting Messiah would suffer, and now, Mark was saying, Jesus had declared his suffering would be central to his ministry, and how God would restore his people.

Rufus inhaled and let out a sigh; it had always been a lot to absorb.

Not that the Torah or the Prophets lacked any hint of a suffering Messiah. Rufus knew that, throughout Scripture, Israel suffered. God empathized with them. The bruised heel of God's end-time deliverer in Genesis came to mind. Daniel's Son of Man, which Mark connected to Jesus, identified with the persecuted Israelites. This should have been nothing new, but tonight, it felt pristine and untainted.

Rufus continued listening with fascination. The descriptions flowed, accumulating strength in his imagination. He compiled questions and observations as he listened. To Rufus, everyone else in the room disappeared.

Mark spoke of the amazing Jesus. In the mysterious event on the mountain, Jesus was substantially and remarkably transformed before the eyes of three disciples. Here again, Mark's portrait broke the mold — presenting a suffering Messiah who ushers in a Kingdom marked by trial.

This grabbed Rufus as important.

Standing with Jesus on the mountain were the stalwarts of Israel, Moses and Elijah. And then, the voice from heaven speaks again, "This is my beloved Son; listen to him."

"Of course," Rufus thought. "The disciples must obey Jesus. Of course." Jesus undermined their common understanding of Messiah. They resisted, and then this massive voice from heaven requires them to listen to him. Who is this man that even God told them to obey?

Jesus healed more, and then he taught. Mark heralded Jesus' teachings about divorce, wealth, and the Kingdom. Jesus invited children to come.

Mark portrayed Jesus as Messiah, one who reaffirmed the expectation of Kingdom living.

Again, Rufus ran ahead of the story. He thought about the poet, prophet Isaiah. Like other prophets of Israel, Isaiah looked back at Israel's Exodus from Egypt. Mark told him and his uncle that Isaiah was also recasting the event as a new prophecy — the victory over both physical and spiritual.

Rufus's attention deepened. Mark evoked surprise and thrill, and Rufus considered each account as Mark read the words from the scroll, always a hint of the old in each new story.

"And they came to Jericho. And as he was leaving Jericho with his disciples and a great crowd, Bartimaeus, a blind beggar, the son of Timaeus, was sitting by the roadside. And when he heard that it was Jesus of Nazareth, he began to cry out and say, 'Jesus, Son of David, have mercy on me!' And many rebuked him, telling him to be silent. But he cried out all the more, 'Son of David, have mercy on me!' And Jesus stopped and said, 'Call him.' And they called the blind man, saying to him, 'Take heart. Get up; he is calling you.' And throwing off his cloak, he sprang up and came to Jesus."

The way Mark recounted this story felt new to Rufus. He'd learned of Bartimaeus before. God was doing a new thing. Conversations overhead between Uncle Ephron and Mark provided clues, and Jesus' identity became clearer. Each story on the road to Jerusalem echoed Peter's affirmation, "You are the Messiah."

Just as Rufus expected, Jesus' identity as King moved into center stage in Mark's story. Bartimaeus twice exclaims "Son of David." How was it he perceived Jesus as the long-awaited king? Did this blind beggar really see Jesus as a Messiah who would reign and bring about wholeness?

Making the blind see was new. Isaiah promised a God who would ransom them from their blindness. Mark recounted it in stories of Jesus. The twist was its refreshing newness. Mark echoed the prophet, "I am doing a new thing; now it springs forth, do you not perceive it? I will make a way in the wilderness and rivers in the desert."

New! Rufus experienced new excitement as Mark read into the night.

"And Jesus said to him, 'What do you want me to do for you?' And the blind man said to him, 'Rabbi, let me recover my sight.' And Jesus said to him, 'Go your way; your faith has made you well.' And immediately he recovered his sight and followed him on the way."

Rufus pulsed with anticipation. Mark's second exodus was to be a definitive, consummate event, earth-shattering in its impact — so cataclysmic that the blind could see, the Messiah would decisively asphyxiate sin, he would forge a remnant, and he would usher in the new heavens and earth that Israel awaited.

Rufus saw a framework that explained Mark's matchless way of talking about Jesus. Many of Jesus' actions that Mark was reporting fit with Isaiah's expectations for this new exodus. Weren't the healings and demon expulsions evidence of that? Now that the new creation has dawned, the Messiah exorcises demons. He heals lepers. The blind can see, the lame can walk, and sinners receive forgiveness. He was beginning a new creation.

Who does these things? Who makes things new?

As a mighty warrior, one who identifies with the God of Israel, Mark was presenting Jesus as the one who would vanquish Israel's true enemy and would guide his people through the wilderness of sin and legalism and into a new future of grace and freedom.

Rufus remembered hearing Mark say, "Upon Israel's arrival in the Promised Land, Yahweh will dwell with his people in a far more glorious way — not in a man-made tabernacle or temple, but rich in the covenant community of his people."

This was the Jesus that Mark was presenting, but it confused Rufus why Jesus had to suffer to accomplish this amazing goal. He understood, but he didn't. The audience's murmurings confirmed the difficulty for them as well. It had been difficult for Peter to believe; it remained a puzzling concept to this moment.

The bewilderment and lack of clarity he was experiencing troubled him.

"Give me sight," Rufus prayed.

THE SCRIBE

In the flickering light, Rufus watched as Mark adeptly used his fingers and wrists to roll the scroll to a new section. He studied the dark shadows on the backside of the parchment, created by the Greek letters written there.

* * *

A couple of weeks earlier, Rufus's uncle had asked him to deliver a satchel of food to Mark.

"Do you remember where he lives?"

His uncle expressed the question with his eyes. Rufus had been there once with Uncle Ephron, although his uncle made him stay outside. Now he was sure he could make his way back there. He had proven himself quite adept at navigating the mishmash of Rome's neighborhoods and districts.

"I'll find it," Rufus assured his uncle. "Don't worry

about me."

"When you get there, leave the man alone. Make the delivery and come back to the shop. Please, Roof, none of your questions today, please."

"Yessir."

Rufus made his way through the narrow corridors to a section of Rome that was a couple of districts to the north. As he walked, he could smell the fire's remnants in the air. He passed two stretches of streets where the fires had completely obliterated the buildings. All that remained were heaps of ashes. Several people were combing through the piles to salvage anything that might have survived.

Arriving at the hovel, which he recognized, he knocked. John Mark yelled for him to enter, and he did.

What he saw shocked him. Mark had a makeshift table of crates and slats that was covered in parchments. Light from a small clay lamp on the corner of the desk was burning wildly because the wick sat too far out of the oil. It revealed a small space with a bed roll against the far wall, which Rufus could probably reach had he tried. There was not much else there besides a small stack of scrolls in the crook near the head of the sleeping mat.

An inkwell made of ginger-colored clay sat at the corner of the longest slat. It was tiny enough to fit into the palm of one's hand. Mark sat, bent over the writing surface, staring at words on the closest parchment. He held a reed between his thumb and forefinger, both of which were blackened by ink. Rufus could smell the fresh *atramentum*, the ink, whose sweet acacia aroma flavored the air of the tiny lean-to. Artisans and scribes made ink from the sap of the acacia tree, mixed with iron vitriol, which supplied its black color.

When Mark turned to greet Rufus, another surprise awaited. He saw Mark's eyes, swollen, reddened, and wet. Soot from the lamp covered his face apart from a couple of damp tracks that rolled from his eyes.

"Ah, young Rufus," he said. "Come in. What have you got there?"

Rufus placed the satchel next to where Mark sat. Despite his uncle's request, a hundred questions surfaced in Rufus's mind, bet he remembered his instructions and held his tongue. Mark took the satchel and unpacked the dried meat, figs, cheese, and bread that Ephron had packed for him.

"I apologize for my mess. My work has preoccupied me these days."

"That's alright, sir. I just came to bring those supplies to you from my uncle."

"Your uncle, Rufus, is a very godly man. I love him so." Mark had swiveled around to face the young man, and he was staring down at the reed in his ink-stained hand.

"Again, I'm sorry. I was just writing a story about my mentor, Peter. It moved me deeply."

Mark wiped the tears from his face, making a mess of the soot. He fiddled with the groceries before him.

"I loved him so much. I'd have done anything for him." Mark spoke of Peter, describing his raisin-colored menace of curls that rose above his smooth olive face.

"His fiery eyes sparkled above his tangled beard." Mark spoke at a deliberate pace. "His shoulders were broad from years of tugging nets in and out of his boat. I wouldn't call him handsome, but I would say he was noticeable."

Mark hesitated and then looked at Rufus.

"He looked worse the first time I saw him. I was a new follower of Jesus; we all were." The cadence of his words increased. "I was visiting my mother's house in Jerusalem. There was a servant girl named Rhoda, who was worshiping with us. She was the only one who heard the knock at the door over the singing and praying. When she went to see who it was, she squealed. Without opening the door, she ran back to the room and yelled, 'Peter's here!' Eventually, someone opened the door. Peter was standing there, a complete mess. It was the first time I ever saw those fiery eyes. Assisted by the angel of the Lord, he had miraculously escaped from his cell. Through further stories he shared about that evening's encounter with Herod and the soldiers. The events were staggering.

"Over the years, Peter and I grew to know each other well. Despite my failures on my first missionary expedition, he embraced me as a son. He was all aboard when I accompanied Barnabas a few years later to Cyprus. I eventually became a close associate of Peter. I would say he made my mother's home his center for ministry. There was always lively fellowship in her house. The butcher shop is the closest thing to it I can think of."

"I love it when you guys come to the shop," Rufus said.

"Me, too, Rufus. Me, too."

Mark described accompanying Peter to Asia Minor and Rome and how he continued with him while he was in prison. Over time, he served as Peter's clerk, taking care of details, and writing letters behind the scenes of Peter's ongoing ministry.

"Peter's Greek was atrocious, not that mine's anything to brag about. I always had to stand in as an interpreter." Mark laughed. "However, the depth of what he shared was always remarkably insightful. Who would have thought a fisher from Galilee would have such keen insight?"

Mark laughed again.

"He called me his son." Tears came again to Mark's eyes.

Rufus watched the man. It did something inside him to see this stalwart in such emotional turmoil. He didn't know what to do or say.

"Those were the days when the Lord Jesus did most of his work in my heart. He transformed me from being a proud, haughty youngster to a lover of good. The transformation was remarkable. I can hardly describe it."

When Mark paused again, Rufus interrupted, though he didn't want to. He could have listened for hours.

"My uncle needs me to get back."

"Be on your way, then. Tell Ephron thanks for me. The Lord uses him."

Rufus left the shack and headed toward the shop.

A flash of shame welled up inside Rufus. It was a mixture of elements pressing on the young man. He felt awkward seeing Mark's raw emotion, and he felt an overwhelming awareness of his own shortcomings. He didn't know what to make of it.

Several weeks earlier, the four friends, Agnus, Rufus, Joshua, and Polonius, were leaning against a column in the marketplace munching on dried fruit. They prattled on about this and that. Rufus strategically leaned close enough for his shoulder to touch Agnus's. Suddenly, Joshua leapt forward and grabbed a piece of fruit out of Rufus's hand and took a big bite out of it.

It angered Rufus, and he ambushed Joshua, pinning him to the ground. By all appearances, he was about to hit him when Agnus and Polonius came to Joshua's rescue. After the two dusted themselves off, the quartet broke up, Joshua and Polonius taking off, and Agnus and Rufus heading toward the shop.

"You get so angry sometimes, Rufus," Agnus spoke. "Joshua was just playing."

Rufus had little to say. Eventually, he muttered, "I

don't want to be like this, but I can't seem to change."

These thoughts filled his mind as he walked home from Mark's. What did he mean when he talked about Jesus doing "most of his work" and the "transformation?" In past butcher shop discussions, Mark had said Jesus came to liberate his people from their sins and bring them into the new creation. What did this mean? What did this mean for him? Rufus longed to know.

MISSION
MOVEMENT

By this time, Mark had rolled most of the scroll into his left hand. Men trimmed the lamps and added oil, while the people listened with passionate ears. Occasionally, someone would sigh or gasp. Clapping erupted at healings, and, as Mark described Jesus' teaching, stillness echoed throughout the tombs.

Rufus observed Jesus and his disciples' movement toward Jerusalem. The opening tales of Mark's parchment happened in the Galilean region. The flow, now, moved him into the capital. Rufus knew the outcome of the story, but Mark's narrative was drawing him into rich themes and affections.

Jesus is king. Do you see? Can you understand? Can you see? Do you not yet understand? The hammering of these phrases battered Rufus's heart. He knew. He understood. In his mind, he did. But did he?

Who do you say that I am?

The prophesied Kingdom would establish God's rule. Rufus's mind flooded with prophetic images. Ultimate destruction of unrighteousness and foreign oppression would precede it. Messiah's arrival would signal the demise of evil. Daniel warned pagan kings that God would crush their kingdoms. The Messiah would shatter them with an iron rod.

Still — the restlessness returned — the assembly gathered in that cave lived in fear. Rome and Nero had the iron rods now. Rufus was straining to connect Mark's Jesus to the reality of centurions and fire burning around him.

"We realize," Rufus thought, "that the Messiah, David's descendant, will establish God's eternal Kingdom and destroy Israel's enemies. Isn't that what we long for? Wouldn't the destruction of Rome now fit that scenario?"

Rufus continued his ruminations. Any such judgment would be decisive. Would it happen at the end of history or not? Despite Jesus coming, dying, and rising from the dead, his Kingdom wasn't as clear as one might assume. Certainly, a complete defeat and judgment of the wicked hadn't occurred.

In Rufus's Rome, two realms coexisted — those belonging to the Kingdom and those belonging to the Evil One. If God had inaugurated his Kingdom in Jesus, he had not yet fulfilled it. Does it exist already? Or was it not yet? Why would Jesus pay taxes to

Caesar?

Healing blind men. Cursing fig trees. Lauding widows. Deriding the scribes. What is this all about? Kingdom or no Kingdom? These questions provoked Rufus. It was a mystery — a new revelation being played out in Mark's manuscript. Would God's Kingdom come in the way Jesus proclaimed? Or would it work among men in a hidden, secret form? Rufus strained to understand.

Somehow, it all came down to the question echoing inside his head.

Who do you say that I am?

"The prophets often used blindness," Rufus's uncle had said to him, "to describe Israel's inability to discern God's revelation." He understood his uncle meant the Israelites couldn't grasp God's actions or his revelation to them. Mark's contrast of Bartimaeus with the religious leaders walloped hard.

Rufus knew by heart the infamous critique found in the writings of Moses, "But to this day, the Lord has not given you a heart to understand or eyes to see or ears to hear." It was a sure indictment of the people. Mark implied that Jesus intended to make the same charge against the religious rulers and perhaps an accompanying warning to those who were his disciples.

As he received Jesus' teaching, Rufus grappled, exploring principles in Mark's thoughts. Why would Israel be in a state of blindness? Bowing down to idols? He turned the exploration on himself.

"Am I, years after Jesus, doing the same?" Rufus thought. These queries pulsed through his imagination. There were frequent arguments at the synagogue about Israel and her state of blindness during Isaiah's day. Today, many thought that she was still in a state of blindness.

Rufus considered each story as Mark read the words from the parchment scroll.

Conversations overhead between Rufus's uncle and John Mark provided clues to where Mark was leading his audience. Jesus' identity became clearer. Each story on the road to Jerusalem echoed Peter's affirmation, "You are the Messiah."

Rufus began a new line of questioning. Why did Mark put Jesus' kingship on display here? What relationship existed between healing the blind and the in-breaking of the Messianic Kingdom?

He remembered his father telling him about John the Baptist being in prison and hearing about the deeds of the Christ. John sent word to Jesus' disciples asking, "Are you the one who is to come, or shall we look for another?"

It was the same question that Mark was provoking in his listeners, and it was the inquiry Rufus was rehearsing in his own thoughts.

Jesus answered John's disciples, "Go and tell John what you hear and see: the blind receive their sight and the lame walk, lepers are cleansed and the deaf hear, the dead are raised up and the poor have good news preached to them." It was all over Mark's gospel — everywhere.

Mark rolled the scroll to a new column and continued.

The gathered group burst into celebration as Jesus entered Jerusalem on a donkey. Several shouted, "Hosanna." This took place on the first day of the last week of Jesus' life. It was the most public event in his ministry. Mark told how Jesus commanded his disciples to find him a specific colt, an unbroken colt that had one mission only — to carry the kingly Messiah. This held another prophecy from the Scriptures.

Then, Mark disclosed how Jesus entered the temple twice. After his victorious entrance to Jerusalem, Jesus made a quick exploratory visit by himself. And then, the following day with his disciples, Jesus "drives out" the money changers from the temple's courtyard.

Mark had already used this verb, "drive out," several times during the evening, each time referring to exorcisms and demons. "Perhaps," Rufus thought to himself, "Jesus' expulsion of the money changers on a physical level was an expulsion of demons on a spiritual level. Jesus' activity begins with an exorcism in Galilee and ends with one in Jerusalem."

Mark recounted Jesus' teaching on the judgment of Jerusalem. This couldn't have sat well with the

Pharisees, who viewed themselves as God's anointed representatives. Rufus wondered if Jesus was preparing the temple so that God might dwell once again with humanity and creation.

The cave was quiet as people reflected on Jesus' mission in Jerusalem.

MISSION
FULFILLED

The mood in Mark's text turned dark. The rulers strategized to quell Jesus' impact. There is confrontation at the temple. An unnerving story followed. An unnamed woman gives the appearance of preparing Jesus for burial, anointing him with expensive perfume.

Next, Mark's narration described Jesus and his disciples celebrating Passover. This was familiar to everyone in the cave, for they had just rehearsed it earlier in the evening. His succinct retelling left the room somber, anticipating Jesus' upcoming death as the Passover sacrifice. This connection rang true to Rufus.

Mark showed that just as God redeemed Israel from Egyptian bondage, Jesus' death would release those in spiritual exile, a theme that Mark loved and expounded upon regularly in the butcher shop dialogues. This theme had become recognizable, but remained mysterious to Rufus.

The ultimate acts of Mark's drama left Rufus with a persuasive portrait of Jesus in his role as Isaiah's servant. Mark was presenting Jesus as the direct fulfillment of Isaiah's expectation of a new Moses to set his people free from slavery by being the Passover lamb.

Although Rufus had listened time and time again to Mark talk about these ideas in the butcher shop discourses, it seemed important now that a disciple must view every story of Jesus' ministry — all these mysterious, amazing, astounding, and radical things — through his death and resurrection. To recognize the end of this story would bring clarity to the beginning and middle portions.

Mark read on.

As Jesus interacted in Jerusalem, Jewish opposition intensified. Everything pointed to the culmination in his death. The series of Jewish confrontations in act one of Mark's gospel now climaxed with an ultimate confrontation that would lead to Jesus' execution.

Rufus and the crowd listened as Mark proceeded.

"And Jesus said, 'For even the Son of Man did not come to be served, but to serve, and to give his life as a ransom for many.'"

Once again Rufus recognized Jesus' wording drawn from the Isaiah scroll:

"Yet it was the Lord's will to crush him and cause

him to suffer,

   and though the Lord makes his life an offering for sin.

My righteous servant will justify many, and he will bear their iniquities.

He poured out his life unto death and was numbered with the transgressors.

   For he bore the sin of many."

The servant songs were prominent in Isaiah's writings. Rufus realized that, through suffering and defeat, Jesus is executing his rule. Rufus fathomed that there might be victory amid defeat; glory amid suffering; and power amid weakness. It was etching slowly into his mind how Mark intended this to be a rich encouragement to the Roman believers in the catacombs that night.

The night slipped on, and with sharp, gut-wrenching intensity, Mark persevered in his reading, highlighting Jesus' identity as Israel's long-awaited King by mentioning several royal features during his mocking and crucifixion: a purple robe, a crown of thorns, the Roman soldiers' taunt "Hail, King of the Jews," and the soldiers' sarcastic genuflecting to the broken man. Rufus, trying to be a careful listener to Mark's narrative, encountered a poignant irony: in mocking Jesus, the soldiers acknowledged his identity as King. They did so unaware.

The words and phrases continued: "And they brought him to the place called Golgotha (which means Place of a Skull). And they offered him wine mixed with myrrh, but he did not take it. And they crucified him and divided his garments among them, casting lots for them, to decide what each should take. And it was the third hour when they crucified him."

The narrative moved Rufus to tears. He rubbed his eyes.

The crucifixion occupied a central place in Mark's narrative. Mark was expecting this event from the very beginning, throughout the middle of the scroll, and now highlighting the end of the story. With scarce words, Jesus proceeded to the scandalous cross as the suffering servant.

Another familiar passage from his upbringing stung at this moment. Rufus recalled the words of the prophet Zechariah. "Rejoice greatly, O daughter of Zion! Shout aloud, O daughter of Jerusalem! Behold, your king is coming to you; righteous and having salvation is he, humble and mounted on a donkey, on a colt, the foal of a donkey."

From the donkey to the cross, Jesus fulfilled the predictions he had made to his disciples. Jesus' identity as God's royal Son was on display at the crucifixion. It was here where Jesus refashioned Israel's expectations of a coming Messiah. Who is this man?

Mark read plainly, "And when the centurion who stood facing him saw that in this way he breathed his last, he said, 'Truly this man was the Son of God!'"

Rufus wasn't sure what to make of the comment.

It felt powerful. He noted that Mark was near the end of the scroll. Even though tired, Rufus was captivated by Mark's writing. Tears fell down his cheeks. Others cried as well.

On most nights, a reading could have rocked him to sleep. Not tonight. This story, this compilation of many tiny stories, read with its rapid-fire staccato, had caused his pulse to quicken. His head spun, his heart pounded, and his eyes spread wide, filled with tears.

After a long pause, Mark read the last column of the scroll.

"When the Sabbath was past, Mary Magdalene, Mary the mother of James, and Salome bought spices, so that they might go and anoint him. And very early on the first day of the week, when the sun had risen, they went to the tomb. And they were saying to one another, 'Who will roll away the stone for us from the entrance of the tomb?'"

Mark halted. The room was like a twig, about to snap. Rufus had moved to his haunches, awaiting the words. Almost every soul was leaning forward, trying to hear the words sooner.

Mark gazed over the parchment. Now, Rufus spotted tears forming in the brown reservoirs of Mark's eyes, reflecting in the oil lamps' dimming light. He admired Mark in that moment — the passion, the stamina, the confidence — it spilled into their world.

He said, "And looking up, they saw that the stone

had been rolled back — it was very large. And entering the tomb, they saw a young man sitting on the right side, dressed in a white robe, and they were alarmed. And he said to them, 'Do not be alarmed. You seek Jesus of Nazareth, who was crucified. He has risen; he is not here. See the place where they laid him. But go, tell his disciples and Peter that he is going before you to Galilee. There you will see him, just as he told you.' And they went out and fled from the tomb, for trembling and astonishment had seized them, and they said nothing to anyone, for they were afraid."

Mark rolled up the scroll. A murmur passed through the audience. The gathering was unsettled. A question hung over the assembly, seeming to inhibit the glut of emotions and reservations that were noticeable from every corner of the cavern. The quietness grew loud in its force.

Yet Rufus was confident — John Mark had sought this exact response.

Who do you say that I am?

Who was Jesus? The women at the tomb had to answer that question; so too each of them sitting in that Roman grotto had to answer it. What was each person's connection with him? Was he Messiah? How would he affect each of them during the trials they faced? What hope did he offer? How were they changed by him? The empty tomb and the confused women kindled the question for Mark's audience.

Who do you say that I am?

After a season of deafening stillness, someone called the assembly to attention. Phoebe and an elder moved to the front of the assembly.

"Oh, Mark," the elder stammered. He appeared wordless in the moment. "Umm, amazing. I don't know what to say. Ah, your words about our astounding Messiah are astonishing — so heartening. Indeed, the Holy Spirit is at work in this work you've done. I can't think of doing anything but offering God our praise."

With that, the elder fell to his knees and poured out a psalm of praise and thanksgiving. Rufus felt touched by the passion of the man's prayer. His heart lifted to join his praise.

The elder rose to his feet and, turning to Mark, said, "May God bless you and any who receive these words."

Phoebe, too, had misty eyes. Rufus longed to know what she felt.

"It's late," she said. "We should disperse. Please leave a few at a time and be careful in the streets. I pray as you go that each of you would join yourself to Jesus."

With that, the assembly ended.

Rufus grabbed his uncle's hand. He had some serious thinking to do.

AFTERMATH OF THE READING

It was late. Despite Phoebe's request, no evidence showed that the gathering might break up soon. Mark leaned back against the stone wall. He looked weary. The crowd buzzed. With a grip on his uncle, Rufus listened to those around him as he moved toward the exit.

"That was remarkable, oh my!"

"What can we say? There's so much there."

"That's a strange ending. There must be more?"

Rufus squeezed his uncle's hand.

"But is it strange?" he asked his uncle. His uncle shrugged.

This ultimate act of John Mark's drama left the listeners with a clear-cut portrait of Jesus. He is the suffering Messiah of Isaiah and Daniel's victorious Son of Man. Rufus gathered Mark's passion and thoughts he'd been hearing for some time in the shop. Mark would say to those who were skeptical, "You can only understand Jesus through his cross and resurrection."

Most times, he would leave discussions about Messiah with that thought. Now he wrote Jesus' complete "life," establishing the pinnacle question, "Who do you say that I am?"

One must interpret all the events of Jesus' mission through these two events. The cross. The resurrection. Only there is his victory clear.

It was as if Mark wished his readers to finish the book and then immediately begin reading it all over again. To grasp the end of the story brings clarity to the beginning and middle. The series of Jewish confrontations in the first act climaxed with one ultimate confrontation.

Some in the crowd celebrated the idea that through suffering and defeat, Jesus was executing his Messianic rule. There was victory during defeat, glory amid suffering, and power during weakness. Overall, the crowd was enthusiastic hearing Mark's story.

Rufus guided his uncle to the entrance of the catacombs. They allowed another family time to make their way east, and then they left, heading west toward the shop.

They were quiet, but Rufus couldn't be still.

"Oh uncle, I'm bursting inside." He broke the silence. "There's so much I want to say. I have so many thoughts and a lot of questions."

"Hush, boy," his uncle said. "We will have plenty of time to talk at home. Now, we must be safe."

They returned home in silence.

"I suggest you get some sleep," his uncle said. "I know you have a lot on your mind. We'll have tomorrow to discuss this."

Rufus knew he was right. They climbed the stairs and fell onto their mats. Rufus couldn't sleep, but he tried. Different strands of Mark's words broke into his consciousness.

When morning light came, Rufus climbed downstairs. An hour later, his uncle joined him. Rufus had heated some porridge and broke some bread. They ate quietly.

Finally, his uncle spoke. "That was quite a night. Did you get any sleep, son?"

"Not really."

"I didn't think you would. So, what do you think?"

Rufus unloaded. "It was amazing. Everything Mark spoke touched me in so many ways."

"I believe it was a Spirit inspired work," Ephron said.

"It was. I want to know Jesus better. Mark used so few words. He said so much. It was special. Rich. Tender. Clear. And so passionate."

Rufus went on without a breath.

"I love how he made the prophets' promises come alive in Jesus. It was incredible how Mark highlighted Jesus' identity as Israel's long-awaited king."

"Listen to you, young man. You are a genuine scholar."

Rufus blushed.

"I'm serious. You're bright, and you pay close attention. You see what most of us don't."

"Come on. Anyway, I want to know if Mark sees Jesus as replacing the temple? Is he preparing the way for an end-time temple where God gathers outcasts and makes them joyful in his presence? You told me the prophets hinted at that."

"Well, yes, it seems to me as if Ezekiel sees a new temple full of God's glory."

"Yes, and think about where Mark showed that God's glory had descended on the Son."

"Yes, but it may be presumptuous to assume God's judgment on the physical temple."

"But Jesus, himself, predicted that, didn't he?"

"Mark inferred that, but I'm not sure."

"Sure, but when Jesus told the parable of the tenants, he was calling out the Pharisees and pointing toward judgment."

"Yes."

"Do you remember Isaiah's song of the vineyard?"

His uncle nodded and watched with a gleam in his

eyes.

Rufus recited the song.

"And now, O inhabitants of Jerusalem
and men of Judah,
Judge between me and my vineyard.
What more was there to do for my vineyard
that I have not done in it?
When I looked for it to yield grapes,
why did it yield wild grapes?
And now I will tell you
what I will do to my vineyard.
I will remove its hedge,
and it shall be devoured;
I will break down its wall,
and it shall be trampled down.
I will make it a waste;
it shall not be pruned or hoed;
and briers and thorns shall grow up;
I will also command the clouds
that they rain no rain upon it."

"Do you see what I mean, Roof?" his uncle said, his chin elevated in delight. "You are a scholar."

They talked a bit more.

"Enough talk, Roof. We need to get our work going. Customers are going to be here anytime. Help me bring in the flank."

NEW TEMPLE

A day later, John Mark appeared at the butcher shop. It delighted Rufus to see him. He appeared worn, as if weighed down by the previous month's writing. Rufus's uncle offered him a glass of wine and some sweet bread. Mark sat on a stool and ate.

"You look tired, my friend," the uncle said.

"It is a good tired, though. I am glad to be sustained by Jesus himself."

With admiration, Rufus watched Mark sip his wine.

"So," said his uncle, "what's the response been to your gospel?"

"It may be too soon to give it a proper assessment, but I feel the initial reaction has been all that I hoped for. I had two goals. I wanted it to encourage the saints, especially as we embrace another season of persecution. It was also my ambition to get those who doubt to reconsider who Jesus is. Being a disciple begins with a recognition that he is Messiah, Son of God, ruler of all creation."

"Very good," said Rufus's uncle.

"It seems from what I've heard that they have received it to this effect."

"I found it encouraging, myself," Rufus said.

"Thank you, Rufus."

"I have a million questions, though."

"Well, perhaps I have time for one."

"That's outstanding."

Rufus's uncle shook his head in awe of the young man. "Silly scholar."

"So, I was just asking my uncle about this. I'm not sure exactly how to ask it."

"Go ahead. We'll get to the question in some fashion."

"Yes. Do you mean to suggest, or did Jesus imply he was replacing the temple? Do you know what I'm asking?"

"A brilliant question, silly scholar, as the old man calls you. Yes, and yes. Based on my talks with Peter, I believe so."

Rufus leaned over the table and rested his elbows on it. He placed his chin on his hands.

"When Moses wrote of Eden in Genesis, he understood Eden was a temple. God walked in the garden with Adam and Eve. He was present with them. Later, the tabernacle and then the temple became the place where God's presence lived among his people. In Eden, life was abundant, and water flowed freely. Unfortunately, sin profaned that sanctuary, causing Adam and Eve to be cast from God's presence."

Rufus drew it all in.

"In that garden," Mark said, "in the presence of God, Adam and Eve were kings, representing God. He said, 'let them rule.' He also told them to work and watch over the garden. In that role, they served as priests, again on God's behalf. The command to 'fill the earth' implies that the earth lacked the right number of images reflecting God's glory. It was a commissioning of sorts."

He continued, "When God chose Israel, he intended the same. His presence lived in the holy of Holies within the temple. But as you know, Israel continued the errant path of their forefathers. The result was sin and separation from God. Over and over, the pattern repeats itself. Peter, taught by Jesus, claimed a new temple was being built through the work of Messiah. Rebellion did not diminish the gracious promise of redemption. Sin corrupted the divine image and infected the created order but did not abolish God's image. He is present now in the Holy Spirit and we are, so to speak, the temples where he is present."

"Unbelievable," Rufus exploded.

"I have vastly oversimplified it, but that is the

cornerstone of my answer. Yes. I implied that in his death, Jesus replaced the temple. And, yes, Peter, my mentor, believed that Jesus had taught that."

"Incredible, simply incredible. It's breathtaking that Jesus identified himself with Daniel's Son of Man rising on the clouds. That's a clear claim to be God. It's no wonder the Pharisees became enraged."

"My dear Rufus, I love your precious heart. The King will use you in mighty ways; he may even use the amazing questions you ask."

Mark looked at him, making eye contact. He invited Rufus to stay connected with his eyes, which he did.

"The incarnation," Mark said, "the life of Jesus, Messiah, God, becoming human, took all that properly belongs to us in our humanity. And do you know what? The incarnation delivered it all back to us, redeemed and complete. All our inclinations, all our appetites, all our capacities, and Jesus purified all our yearnings and gathered them up for his glory."

Rufus listened, absorbed in the imagination of Mark's idea.

"He did not come," Mark said, "to make human life thin and insignificant; He came to set it free. All the eating and working and living and celebrating, all the tent making and sculpting, the designing, and the commemorating — all that belongs to humanity, and that Satan stole away into his service and that of his false gods — they come back to life, full as ever, in the gospel."

Rufus's uncle threw up his hands.

"Mark, you are too much. You are going to mess this young man up with your grandiose imagination," he teased. "He must cut meat. He's a butcher, and right now he needs to mop the floor. Rufus, you've asked your one question; it's time to work."

"God redeems even butchers, my good friend," said John Mark. "There is nothing finer than one of your lamb shanks. Now, let the young man dream."

Mark made his way to the door. He nodded and slipped out. Rufus followed him, watching him go.

As Mark waved goodbye, he half-yelled, "Jesus is king."

Rufus nodded, waved back, and shut the wooden door. That was a bold exclamation to make on the street. Mark was a bold man. Rufus smiled.

PERSECUTION INTENSIFIES

Days later, Rufus and Agnus were walking down the same alley where they had rescued her mother's cart. They neared the agora's entrance, and a voice behind yelled.

"What are you doing?"

Neither of them looked. They heard hurried thuds of the heavy sandals behind them. Rufus pushed Agnus on and slowed his gait. She kept going as a centurion stepped past Rufus, turning, and confronting him.

"Where are you going?"

"I am delivering meat for my uncle."

"I know you. You're the Jew in charge of the group the other day."

Rufus recognized the centurion who had led the confrontation on the plaza.

"I was in the group corralled by your legion, sir, but I was not in charge."

Rufus looked over the epaulet on the soldier's shoulder, seeing Agnus up the alley. She made distance but turned to watch. She wrinkled her brow with concern.

"I told you not to gather," the centurion barked.

"As I told you, sir, I am making deliveries." He swung the satchel from his back and opened it for examination.

"Don't be insolent with me, young man." Rufus didn't think the centurion could be much older than himself. "You aren't in any position to speak to me that way."

"I am sorry, sir. I was only telling you the truth."

"What is truth?"

The centurion bored through him with his eyes, and it unsettled Rufus.

"You Jews are so concerned with truth, especially the ones called Christians."

The intensity of the moment made it difficult for Rufus to keep his head up.

"I warn you. Do not let me catch you again. You are in danger. There is an edict from the emperor to gather Christians for arrest. Don't let me see you again. Now go make your deliveries."

Rufus stepped around him and resumed his path. Agnus was nowhere in sight. He wondered if the centurion knew he was a follower of Jesus. Did he know anything else? What if he had asked him? Would Rufus have answered him truthfully?

That night at the gathering, the discussion was frantic. Earlier, the Roman Guard arrested two of their members. Officials knew them to be followers of the way and nabbed them in the forum.

Persecution was growing, and significant concern emerged that it had approached their doorstep. What was to be done?

Someone argued that there was nothing to be concerned about. The arrest of their compatriots was unfortunate, but unrelated. They claimed that the current policy towards Christians did not differ from the treatment that other religious sects were receiving. They would only punish people if they refused to worship the emperor and the gods.

"This may be true," Phoebe said, "but we should remain vigilant and be safe."

The crowd stirred further, not finding assurance in her words.

"You would refuse to worship the emperor," Mark said. "This isn't the first time Christians were the targets of persecution because they refused to worship the Roman gods or to pay homage to the emperor as divine."

Rufus had heard lectures from his uncle about refusing to sacrifice to the emperor or the empire's gods. Rufus knew this was tantamount to refusing to swear an oath of allegiance to the country. It meant certain death, a death that many had already experienced.

More muttering shook the cave. Rufus couldn't help but wonder about his father. Had he refused some sort of demand to bow to Caesar?

Someone expressed a desire to return to the tenets of Judaism and abandon belief in Jesus. There was already an edict of tolerance between the Jews and Caesar.

"He's obviously not Messiah, or Rome couldn't destroy us like this."

Mark spoke, the veins in his necked elevated. "We must not go back to old ways. The Pharisees misplaced their lust for the Torah. They intended to earn God's favor with their flattened restrictions and adherence to tradition. We must guard the faith. Only by believing in Jesus will we experience genuine hope and unencumbered freedom. We must press on."

"But we are being killed!" a man to his left yelled.

"Yes. Hear, hear." The voices of the crowd trumpeted rage and concern, and the cavern resonated frustration.

"Our hope is in greater realities. Jesus was the pioneer in this; he told us the way would be difficult, then he modeled it for us on the cross."

"Our allegiance is to God," a woman shouted. She was in the back.

"To God alone," another yelled.

Rufus turned to his uncle. "Uncle, I told you about what happened today while I was making deliveries."

"Yes," his uncle said.

"What would happen if the centurion pressed me about being Christian?"

A man standing nearby overheard Rufus.

"Son, I have seen horrible things done to Christians by the Romans."

He explained he had worked for a rich Roman merchant and had been in the background on three specific occasions where Roman soldiers had pressed believers. They interrogated them whether they were Christians. Those who confessed they interrogated a second and a third time. The soldiers threatened them with punishment.

"I watched as they beheaded one man for refusing to reject Christ. One woman, poor lady, rejected Christ under intense pressure from the soldiers. They forced her to prove allegiance to the Roman gods by reciting phrases the soldiers dictated to her and swearing allegiance to the emperor by drinking wine to his image. She was so frightened. It was sad."

Rufus looked at his uncle.

"I swear to you: they couldn't force any of those who are genuinely Christians to do this. Soldiers tortured the other man, but at no point would he deny his Messiah. That man is one reason I follow Jesus today."

The noise grew until an elder yelled for the crowd's attention.

"I warn you," Phoebe said, when it grew quiet. "We have a greater enemy than Caesar and Rome."

"That's right," Mark said, "even in Jesus' day, there was an expectation that the Messiah would be a political deliverer. Time will come when he delivers politically, and he will reign. But for now, he came to free us from sin's effect. The resurrection deems Jesus' work victorious over Satan, sin, and the world. Jesus' life, death, and resurrection have liberated us — his new covenant community — from sin and estrangement from God."

"It is true," a man yelled from the front of the room.

Mark beckoned to his listeners to believe this message, and to join the redeemed.

"We, the redeemed, trust that the Messiah will be faithful to his promises. The resurrection makes this certain. Who do you say that he is?"

Mark surveyed the gathering.

"Death will not triumph over these promises. I beg you to persevere. Press into Jesus and experience his grace."

The group prayed, sang spiritual songs, and encouraged each other before they dispersed.

THE PROJECT

"**F**ollow me," John Mark said.

The men followed deeper into the cavern to a dimly lit room.

"Friends," Mark said. His eyes were tired and lonely. "I have little time. I must go. Paul has summoned me again, for he has some need for me. I'm not sure what, but I must go. I fear his death is imminent. Meanwhile, it's imperative that this scroll makes it to the gatherings in as many cities as possible. You will be crucial to this. Let me explain."

There were twelve young men gathered around Mark. His friend Joshua was one of them. Rufus recognized most of them from the gathering. There were a couple that Rufus had seen but never met.

Mark continued. "We must get these stories of the Master to more people. I have recorded with accuracy what Peter told me about Jesus. I did not hear the Lord myself nor follow him during his life, but afterward I followed Peter. Peter would teach often about his experiences with Jesus. He conformed his teaching to the audience and their needs. I attempted to compile here those ideas as I remembered them. I was careful not to leave out anything that I had heard, and not to say anything erroneously. These words must go to God's people scattered about."

The men nodded in agreement. The weeks since the reading had created quite a charged atmosphere among the Roman believers. This, combined with growing persecution and even a few members from the gathering missing, confirmed the need to spread the gospel's encouragement — Jesus is the long-awaited Messiah.

"I have gathered you because of your reputation among the brothers and sisters."

Curiosity had them at this comment. They leaned into Mark's words.

"What I am about to propose to you is risky and dangerous, but I feel it is imperative."

He looked around the group. He looked them in the eyes. When Rufus felt the intensity of Mark's gaze, it gave him courage.

"We will divide the scroll into twelve sections. Each of you will have a section. You may cut it into columns if you choose. These pieces will be your responsibility."

The picture of cutting up Mark's scroll reminded Rufus of the pages he had seen in the shop. They were small square pieces of parchment. Scrawled on each were instructions in his uncle's flowing handwriting. There were drawings of sheep and cows split into pieces. The butcher had loosely attached the pieces of parchment at the corner, forming a portfolio for instructing the shop's apprentices. His uncle was trying to replace the butcher's scroll because of several problems that limited its function and its readability while working in the shop. For one, scrolls were very long, sometimes as long as ten meters. They were difficult to hold open and read while working. He remembered one set of parchments where his uncle had attempted to stitch one side of several sheets and bind it with a thicker piece of cow's hide. It worked, but his uncle decided attaching at the corner was easier for keeping a page open when working. "It is best," his uncle said, "if an apprentice would learn the cuts so they don't have to rely on the instructions."

Now, John Mark was suggesting a dissection for a different purpose — the efficient transport of the gospel that he had written to other places. It was ingenious.

"I have chosen you for another reason — your intellect. It is critical that each of you memorize your section. Should something happen to the scroll, you will still be able to perform your mission."

The men looked at each other. What task is Mark talking about? What consequences and cost?

"One more thing," Mark continued, "you must tell no one about this. No one."

That made Rufus shudder. He vacillated between fear and excitement. His palms were sweating, and his nerves swam with anticipation.

Rufus had longed to travel. Even though everything and everyone passed through Rome, the center of the universe, he itched to know about the rest of the world. Stories of Greece and Mesopotamia always fascinated him. When Mark spoke of Jerusalem, he was in awe. What man of Jewish roots wouldn't want to see Zion? Who wouldn't want to walk where Jesus walked? This might be a dream come true.

The idea held Rufus in a trance of fascination — from Jesus to John Mark to Rufus and these men. Mark's restoration to useful ministry in the church may have been, in part, because of the ministry of Peter. Rufus knew of Peter's close relationship with Mark from listening to him in the shop and at his home. It was clear from his descriptions that Peter had a great impact on him. Rufus remembered the time when Mark shared with sniffles that Peter would talk to him and say, "Mark, my son."

Rufus appreciated that Peter, himself, was no stranger to failure. His influence on the younger Mark was no doubt instrumental in helping him out of the instability of his youth and into the strength and maturity he would need for the work to which God had called him.

That strength and maturity were now calling these twelve individuals into the greater mission of proclaiming the Kingdom of God.

As Mark laid out his directions for the men, Rufus thought of so many things. Was his uncle aware of what Mark was thinking? Would he know Mark had selected him? What would he tell others if they asked about it? What would it be like? So much to think about. Rufus caught enough of Mark's vision to be ready.

Athos, a smaller Greek from Rufus's district, had a lot of questions, too. He verbalized them, showering Mark with requests for where, when, what, why, and how. Joshua looked across to Rufus and rolled his eyes.

Twelve young men stood before Mark. Two of the gentlemen were older than the others, Tryphaena and Tryphosa. Rufus knew about them; they had worked alongside Paul at different points. The others included Joab, Athos, Joshua, Rufus, Caleb, Nathan, Jamin, Lucius, Marcus, and Artemis. Together, the twelve of them gathered around as Mark rehearsed his proposal.

He laid the plan before them. For the next three weeks, the scroll would stay intact. The twelve young men would meet in rotations of four each day. They would arrive by themselves at the catacombs. It was important for them to move in small groups so as not to attract attention. When they met, they would roll the scroll out to a predetermined section.

On the first day of execution, Rufus arrived at his appointed time. No one was at the catacombs. After a brief wait, Mark and one of the other young men, a youth named Artemis, appeared. Next, Joshua came with a man named Caleb. Rufus knew him.

"I have already divided the scroll into sections," Mark said. "There are tiny notations along the bottom edge of the parchment that show the section breaks. Twelve sections. I will assign each part to one of you or your peers."

The men listened, nodding in agreement.

"Rufus, would you memorize the section beginning right after Peter confesses Jesus is the Christ? Keep memorizing all the way to the part where Jesus heals the boy with the unclean spirit, the one the disciples couldn't cast out."

"Yes," Rufus said, "that'll be fine."

"Joshua, please take the next section."

Rufus looked over the parchment.

"They went on from there and passed through Galilee."

Rufus tried to recall Mark's presentation. He knew Jesus left Galilee and traveled to Jerusalem.

"Joshua, you will study through the story when Jesus interacts with the wealthy young man." Mark paused and laughed. "Ah, look around me — a handful of rich young men. What is their response to the Messiah?"

This puzzled Rufus. He didn't consider himself wealthy by any means.

Joshua beat him to the question. "What do you mean? We're not rich."

"But you are," Mark said. "Your families have

assimilated into Roman culture. Your fathers and mothers own shops or work. You have homes. You may not be kings or queens living in palaces, but you have much — more than many. Be grateful, my young companions. Be grateful."

Artemis and the other youth received their assignments. The scroll was unrolled across the floor to the relevant section. The men gathered around it and searched for the tiny marks that showed their sections. They began their studies. Mark produced a handful of figs for the men to chew on as they studied and memorized.

As Rufus began, he brushed his forefinger against the edge of the papyrus. It cut him. With a quick instinctive reaction, he pushed his finger against the scroll.

"What are you doing, Rufus?" Artemis asked.

Startled, Rufus pulled his hand back as if he'd touched a pot hanging over a fire.

They all looked at a red blotch at the bottom of Rufus's section of the scroll.

"Hmmm, aren't we off to a good start, team?" Joshua said.

They looked at each other and laughed.

AGNUS AND THE CENTURION

"**I**'m not sure that I want you to go."

Agnus gave him those guppy eyes that tenderized him. Agnus was one of the few outside the twelve and Mark who was aware of the mission. Her father and mother, being instrumental in the church's leadership, were part of the original planning.

"It will be dangerous. Besides, we need you, and your uncle needs you."

"But Agnus, it's an amazing opportunity — the chance to experience unknown places."

"Do you need to see different places?" Agnus cut him off. "You need to be here."

Rufus often labored when people, especially strong women, spoke sternly. He looked down at the red clay tile below his feet. He was unsure how to handle her emotions. Breathing in, he looked up into her eyes.

"This is important," Rufus said to her. "Mark's vision for encouraging the church and reaching others with the gospel of Jesus Christ is so essential. You understand this."

Agnus looked away.

"You know that my mother died during my birth," Rufus said. "It sent my dad into a tailspin for years. When we came to Rome and when he met your folks, everything changed. Jesus healed my dad. It was the greatest thing that's ever happened. I mean it."

Agnus nodded, watching the emotion surge from Rufus.

"All I can remember from most of my childhood is that my dad was angry about everything. I am sure it was because he was mad about my mother's death. Anything could set off an explosion."

"I'm sorry, Rufus. That must have been rough."

"Thanks, but I don't tell you that to have you feel bad for me." He paused and took in a gulp of air. "When we came to Rome, one of the first people he met was your father. There is nothing more strategic for a tanner than knowing a tentmaker."

"I was too young to remember that," Agnus said, "but your father is part of my earliest memories. I don't recall him being angry."

"That's my point. When father wasn't working, we spent all our extra time in your parent's workplace. All they did was talk about Jesus, the Messiah."

"That's still all my mother and father talk about."

"It changed my father forever."

At this, both Agnus and Rufus paused. Misty eyed Rufus went on.

"As a follower of Jesus, he changed. Right in front of my little boy eyes, he changed. He softened. Nah. That's not the right word. He deepened. Something inside him produced a new strength in him. He was different because of Jesus."

"It must have been amazing," Agnus said. "Rufus, I want to hear more, but we need to get going."

"You're right, we do."

They grabbed the pile of pelts, turned, and resumed their walk back to the shop.

As they walked, Rufus told perhaps the most significant story. He spoke of a time as a teen, when he and his father were walking home from the gathering. Rufus's father scooped the young man into his arms.

"I wiggled in resistance. I was too old to be held by my father. He held me firmly, squeezing me and staring into my eyes. He looked long and with burning intensity."

Rufus remembered seeing the tears welling up behind his father's cocoa brown orbs.

"My father spoke tender words of apology to me, lamenting the hurt he must have caused me by his anger. He made an oath that things would change.

Over time, they did."

Agnus grabbed his hand as they walked, making it somewhat difficult for Rufus to hold on to the pelts. He didn't mind. It was a small price to pay for having Agnus hold his hand.

"I'll never forget it," Rufus said. "Never. Jesus changed my father forever. This is one reason this mission is so vital. Others need to hear about our Messiah. He will change them."

"I believe he will," Agnus said. And then, releasing Rufus's hand, she added, "I just don't want you to go."

"I understand what you are telling me."

They continued in silence as they returned to the butcher shop. Rufus and Agnus hadn't been there long when a knock at the door startled them.

AWKWARD
CONFRONTATION

R ufus answered the door, thinking, "That's strange. Customers know to enter the shop. Why a knock?"

As the door opened, the sight of a centurion smashed Rufus. It was the very centurion who collected the crowd in the plaza and accosted him in the alley. Behind him stood two soldiers at attention with their spears across their chests.

"Whose shop is this? Where is your license?"

Rufus's uncle wasn't there when he and Agnus returned.

The government requires all Roman shops to have a license. It was an engraved piece of marble displayed publicly in the business. It was permissible for a shop to be operated by a family member or a slave who belonged to the owner of the shop, but the license was mandatory.

"This shop belongs to my uncle, Ephron bar Jonas," Rufus said. Did the centurion recognize him? He wasn't sure. "My uncle's not here now. He has gone to the *forum boarium*."

The city fathers converted an ancient market on the outskirts of Rome into an area for cattle grazing. The *boarium* served as the largest cattle market in Rome, perhaps the world. His uncle would go there to purchase bulls and cows to slaughter for their customers.

Rufus pointed across the room to a small wooden shelf attached to the mud wall. Upon it sat a gray piece of marble with a mottled face etched into it and inked with black.

"The license is there, on the shelf."

The centurion examined the stone. He grunted approval, turning to the young man.

"I know you. You're one of those people causing problems in the streets the other day."

This was the second time the centurion had confronted him about the situation in the marketplace. Rufus held his tongue for a moment.

"Yes, I was there. However, I wasn't causing problems. I was only working for my uncle."

Rufus knew that contradicting a centurion was dangerous. The centurion glared at him. His two companions stepped toward Rufus. The centurion waved them back.

"I saw you again in the alley," Rufus continued his explanation. "I was making deliveries for his shop, this shop."

"That is what you told me, but I know your kind."

Rufus stepped forward and with purpose. He looked into the soldier's eyes.

"You asked me, 'What is truth?'"

"I did," the centurion snapped back. He stared back.

"Truth is everything I have. When I speak to you about my work, I can only offer you what I know to be accurate. Apart from that, I am nothing. It matters a great deal to me. I tell you what is true."

The centurion glanced away as if a sword had bounced off his breastplate. Rufus observed his reaction. He stared closer into the man's face and confirmed he wasn't much older than he was.

"Do you have something to drink?" the man asked, pulling himself back to attention. It was mandatory to meet the demands of Roman soldiers. Agnus quickly ran to the cabinet and produced a bottle of wine and three clay cups. Filling the cups, she offered them to the centurion. He took one and nodded to the other soldiers to take one as well.

"Leave us," he said to the soldiers. They walked outside with their cups, shutting the door. The centurion removed his helmet and took a sip of the wine.

"So, truth is special to you?"

"It is," Rufus replied.

"Humph. I often ask that question. 'What is truth?' Most people are liars. Your response is markedly different. You told me you're Jewish. Is that true?"

"It is."

The centurion paused in thought. Rufus and Agnus remained quiet.

"Have you ever been to Israel?"

"I was born there. I came to Rome with my father when I was five."

"I see."

The centurion seemed to soften a bit. Without his helmet, he was slightly less intimidating. He stood there, clearly lost in his thoughts.

"I've asked to be sent to Israel for a tour of duty."

He stopped again and looked over Rufus's shoulders as if he could see the far shores of the Mediterranean. The pause seemed forever.

"That question," the centurion said. "It haunts me. 'What is truth?' It's ridiculous. I heard it from my uncle. He told me one of the most bizarre stories. I've never forgotten it. Like I said, it torments me."

Both Agnus and Rufus stood watching, shocked by the transformation they were seeing.

"My uncle was a teenager when he enrolled in the Roman legion. After training, they assigned him to the Judean region. He spent much time in Jerusalem. In fact, he was at the execution of this man the Jews call Jesus. The centurion of my uncle's legion believed that there was something unique and significant about this man called the Christ.

"During his trial, the governor asked him, 'What is truth?' He stood there without answering, as if the answer was him. My uncle told me how remarkable it was.

"Pilate, the governor, charged my uncle's legion to execute him by crucifixion. And when they were standing there, facing him fixed to the cross, when they saw how he breathed his last, my uncle's commander stood there and said to my uncle and to the other soldiers around him, 'Truly this man was the Son of God!'"

Rufus remembered Mark's story of the crucifixion.

"Later in the barracks, they mocked the words of that centurion. Of course, they never would've done that to his face. Whatever — my uncle never forgot that event. He must have told me the story a hundred times."

The centurion paused. There seemed in him an uncertainty whether he should have told the story.

Rufus hesitated to say anything.

"What do you think of that, butcher?" His gruffness had returned.

"With all due respect to your authority and position as a representative of Caesar, may I say one thing?"

The centurion stared him down. Rufus peered back at the armored man.

"Sir, consider one thing," Rufus said. "Who was this Jesus that your uncle saw, and his centurion venerated? Who was he really? When Jesus stood before the governor accused, in that moment are we not reminded of the accusation that we ourselves justly deserve because of our wrongs? Perhaps Jesus remained silent before the governor so that ever after, he might speak for us. I believe that what is true is that we deserve the judgment he received, yet he did not defend himself, even though he rightfully could have. He stood condemned in my place. It is said that this Jesus took our judgment, and we receive freely the gift of acquittal. I believe that is truth."

With this, Rufus paused, not yet letting go of the lock he had on the soldier's eyes.

Rufus continued, "I ask you to consider one thing like your uncle's commander considered: who do you say he was?"

The centurion stepped forward, lifting his cup toward the counter. Rufus watched Agnus while the centurion set the cup down and remounted his helmet. Regardless of the centurion's take on Rufus's words, reflecting on the magnanimous love of God as shown by Jesus moved Rufus's heart with fresh wonder.

The centurion turned to leave. With a tug on the door, he turned to the pair. With coarseness, he made his parting known.

"I will give your words some consideration. I do not know your connection with the group known as 'the Way,' but I warn you, young butcher, it is a bad time for those people. The emperor has earmarked them for death. You should be careful, both of you."

Agnus grabbed Rufus's hand and squeezed it, tugging him closer to her.

Rufus squeezed back, knowing then that he would undertake Mark's astounding project.

MEMORIZING

And so, the project began. Each man would lay or crouch over his section and begin the business of weaving the words into their brains and their hearts. As they crowded around the parchment, the smells of the spices in the tombs mixed with the breath of the laboring youth made a distinctive scent.

The three who learned in Hebrew schools knew the value of parchment, the writing effort, and the work involved putting a scroll together. They had great respect for the piece in front of them. Coupled with their esteem for John Mark and the undertaking of spreading the gospel, they found themselves in awe.

The project thrilled Rufus. His uncle was in on the plan and excused him from his duties at the shop anytime necessary. Rufus worked all the harder when he was there, knowing the sacrifice his uncle was making.

They exerted great diligence at the job of

memorizing Mark's work.

When he was a boy, Rufus had developed his own style for memory work. It profited him. The expectation in school had been to memorize large sections of the Torah, the Law. To do this, he had to figure out a system to simplify the process. He applied it to the scroll in front of him.

"For he was teaching his disciples, saying to them." He would look carefully at each word as he read. Ten times he read it.

Next, he would close his eyes and repeat the phrase to himself. "For he was teaching his disciples, saying to them." He would repeat that ten times.

Finally, he would open his eyes and read the line out loud. He was checking his retention. "For he was teaching his disciples, saying to them."

He would move on to the next line and repeat the process.

Ten times reading. "The Son of Man is going to be delivered into the hands of men."

Ten times with his eyes closed. "The Son of Man is going to be delivered into the hands of men."

Once out loud. "The Son of Man is going to be delivered into the hands of men."

Then, he would read both lines together. "For he was teaching his disciples, saying to them, the Son of Man is going to be delivered into the hands of men."

Then the next section.

"And they will kill him. And when he is killed, after three days he will rise."

He did this until he had a paragraph memorized.

Ten times reading.

Ten times with his eyes closed.

Once out loud.

Then everything so far.

"For he was teaching his disciples, saying to them, the Son of Man is going to be delivered into the hands of men, and they will kill him. And when he is killed, after three days he will rise."

With those thoughts on his mind, he walked back to the shop. He hoped to get back in time to help his uncle with the day's last chores.

Why would Israel's long-awaited Messiah come and allow himself to be killed? This seemed odd. And the prediction of the resurrection? It was also so mysterious and so amazing.

"The disciples must have been so confused," Rufus thought as he arrived at the shop.

Rufus pushed against the wood and shoved the door open. He set his satchel on the counter, tracing his finger across the stitching that held the bag together. He contemplated the pattern of in and out made by the thread.

"What are you thinking about?" his uncle said.

"Am I in any better position to understand why Mark emphasized Jesus' instructions to stay quiet? He said that to everybody."

"Well, that's an interesting thing to be thinking. I thought you might think about Agnus or dinner. You know, something tangible."

"I suppose," Rufus said. He was listening to his thoughts and not his uncle's.

Truth be told, Rufus himself was reworking his understanding of Messiah. Suffering and death marked the Kingdom and Jesus' messiahship, not political triumph. What did that mean? How did it make sense in Rufus's life and world? Was he afraid of dying?

His uncle interrupted his thoughts again, handing him a list scrawled on a scrap of wood.

"Rufus, please pick up these things at the forum."

Today, Rufus was glad to run his uncle's errand. It gave him more time to reflect on the mishmash of his thoughts. He walked the distance to the center of Rome. He passed the staging area where carriages and horses lined the outside gates. The city prohibited carriages during the day.

The Roman Forum, a larger version of the square in his district, was bustling. The clatter of voices, squawks, and rattling crates rose into the air, still obscure with smoke. Pedestrians crossed in every direction. Slaves carried wealthy Romans in litters throughout.

The Roman architect, Vitruvius, had designed the forum. Rufus's uncle said Vitruvius called the plaza ideal. It was Vitruvius' opinion that a forum should be large enough to accommodate a large crowd, but not so large as to dwarf a small one. It was his belief also that the perfect ratio for one should be three lengths by two breadths. The *agora* in Rufus's district was a miniature version of the same proportions.

The white colonnades contrasted the myriad of colors in the wares, the fruits and vegetables, and the people. Many nationalities moved through the plaza, purchasing all kinds of products, including those from far-away lands.

With the list filled, Rufus crossed the tile pavement. As he moved toward the gates, he spotted Artemis walking his way. They made eye contact and continued walking. They passed each other without acknowledgment. It felt awkward to Rufus, but he understood. He trekked back to the shop with his uncle's goods in hand.

As he walked, he reflected. For years, Rufus had catalogued different passages and ideas from Isaiah, Ezekiel, and the other prophets. He scrambled to recall passages referring to the coming Messiah. It was apparent Mark had connected the great passages of Isaiah with the man, Jesus.

Who was this man? What was the connection that Mark made between Isaiah and Jesus? He had already confirmed to Rufus the connection was there, but the more he read and studied, the more he saw. Was he truly the man of sorrows who bore our grief? Could he have been the one stricken by the transgressions of his people? Was this the same Son of Man whom Daniel forecasted to be the supreme authority over the whole earth? Rufus was confident Mark made this connection in his scroll.

The following day, Rufus, Joshua, Artemis, and Caleb met again.

"I saw you at the Forum yesterday," Artemis said. They rolled out the scroll to work.

"You as well. I wanted to say something. I had spent all day in a funk, speculating about Jesus and what Mark told us about him. It would have been good to talk to you."

"We can talk now."

Talk they did. They worked for three or four hours, discussing everything they were thinking, before returning to their regular occupations. Rufus returned to the butcher's shop. They repeated this daily.

On the last day of the week, the Sabbath, rather than memorize — work — they simply recited what they had learned.

Artemis, being a Gentile believer, asked about the Sabbath laws. A brief discussion ensued. Artemis was glad for the respite from the intense memorization process.

On the first day of the week, the Lord's Day, as they called it, they didn't meet or memorize at all. Instead, most of the twelve attended the gathering. As they saw each other, they neither acknowledged the others nor mentioned anything about their project.

The following day, they would meet again and resume their study and memorization.

INTENSE STUDY

Every so often, John Mark would visit them while they worked. He would ask them how they were doing, and then he would quiz them on sections of their memory work.

"Very good," he said. "That sounds like something I would say."

They laughed.

He would chat with them about family and life. Like his cousin Barnabas, who was renowned for his encouragement, John Mark emboldened each of the young men as they toiled.

"Men," he would say, "God designed us to conquer. He made us to risk. Created us to sweat and face resistance. We should hunt souls, share the gospel with districts, accomplish Jesus' mission — and a hundred other worthy pursuits — in the name of King Jesus. So come, let us go out — the Lord will work for us."

Mark inspired them. From the first time Rufus met Mark in his uncle's shop, Mark's passion and enthusiasm aroused something inside him. His uncle said, "You come away from talking with Mark either fired up or enraged. There was no middle ground." Rufus and his cohort were always "fired up" when he left.

Rufus applied himself and his method to the rest of his section.

He memorized the portion where Jesus exhorted the disciples to deny themselves and take up the cross. When he read the words, they startled him anew. "For whoever is ashamed of me and of my words in this adulterous generation, of him will the Son of Man also be ashamed when he comes in the glory of his Father with the holy angels." This felt harsh to Rufus. What if the centurion had asked him about Christ?

This question caused him to contemplate his own standing with Jesus. He perceived himself to be young in his faith. Even now, as he worked with John Mark, it seemed so new and what he had known seemed so shallow.

Rufus studied the next section. God transfigured Jesus before his disciples and his clothes became radiant, vivid white. This passage had moved Rufus when Mark read it. He thought anew about the voice from heaven.

Next, he memorized the failure of the disciples to cast out a demon.

The crowd's great amazement when Jesus did.

All things are possible with God.

The faith of the boy's father, "I believe, help my unbelief!" Rufus repeated the prayer for himself, "I believe, help my unbelief."

Near the end of the week, Rufus read ten times, "For he was teaching his disciples, saying to them, 'The Son of Man is going to be delivered into the hands of men, and they will kill him. And when he is killed, after three days he will rise.'"

He closed his eyes and said it to himself ten times. "For he was teaching his disciples, saying to them, 'The Son of Man is going to be delivered into the hands of men, and they will kill him. And when he is killed, after three days he will rise.'"

Now, opening his eyes, he read it out loud. "For he was teaching his disciples, saying to them, 'The Son of Man is going to be delivered into the hands of men, and they will kill him. And when he is killed, after three days he will rise.'"

Rufus paused, acknowledging the significance of Jesus repeating this thought. Rufus again wrestled with the idea that the Messiah had to suffer. After all, he was God.

He went on. He read ten times. "But they did not understand the saying, and were afraid to ask him."

He closed his eyes and repeated it ten times. "But they did not understand the saying, and were afraid to ask him."

He said it out loud with eyes wide open. "But they did not understand the saying, and were afraid to ask him."

Rufus wondered about the men and their lack of understanding. He pondered his own strains to wrap his mind around Messiah. Sometimes all he could do was let the experience of knowing Jesus wash over him. It astounded him.

Over the next several days, Rufus finished memorizing his section.

If anyone would be first, he must be last.

The man doing mighty things in Jesus' name.

The wretched temptations to sin and the harsh resolution to cast out anything causing it.

Hard sayings about divorce.

Jesus invites the little children to come to him. For to such belongs the Kingdom of God.

Joshua reclined next to Rufus, applying himself to his section. He read about the rich young man. Joshua had adopted a similar method to memorize the words. It came easier for Joshua.

After that story, Joshua memorized Jesus' prediction of his death.

"Rufus, do you see this passage here?" Joshua asked.

"Which one?"

"Here. This one where Jesus talks about going up to Jerusalem, where they will deliver him over to the council to die? It's somewhat intense."

"Incredible!"

"Incredible? What do you mean, 'Incredible?'"

"Yes, that would make three times Jesus predicted his death in Jerusalem."

"It must have been important to repeat it three times," Joshua said.

"Yes. Well, we know it was. His death is life to us."

Artemis spoke up. "I'm glad for it. It is of the utmost importance, isn't it?"

"Listen to this," Joshua said. "'And they were amazed, and those who followed were afraid.' It must have been something to walk those early days with this radical man."

They all nodded in agreement.

"I'd say it still is," said Caleb. "It's still exciting to walk with this radical man."

Again, they all nodded. And laughed. Rufus laughed as well, but caught himself wondering about what they were getting into — where would Mark's project take them?

The intense memorization process forced careful meditation. The attentive contemplation gave the young men rich opportunities to ruminate on the texts in front of them. Each saw things they hadn't heard when Mark read it to the church. They dared to imagine the impact that it would have when read abroad.

By the middle of the second week, Rufus had his

entire section memorized. He would spend their times together repeating the passage over and over. Artemis was struggling, but working harder than all of them. Joshua had finished and, like Rufus, was repeating his section over and over. Caleb was finishing his part.

The next day, Mark appeared early during their session. With a series of questions, he assessed their readiness for the mission.

"Artemis," John asked, "will you be finished by the start of next week?"

"Yes, sir, I believe I will."

"Athos is also having a hard time. You both received tough sections. But if it's the case, you'll be ready. We will begin the next phase and get you men on your way."

They looked at one another with concern and anticipation. This is it.

"Words cannot express my heartfelt appreciation for you hard work and willingness to undertake this mission."

THE KNIFE

Roman society, like most, divided itself into various social classes. Rufus was aware of this, being the dependent of a merchant. He lived with his uncle in a small space above the shop, a wooden structure with hardened mud packed between the timbers. The hardened walls were solid, like the Roman social class structure. This class consciousness commingled with a restless unease in the plaza down the street from the shop. Rich people and poor people alike crowded the square while going about their daily business, each avoiding the other as much as possible.

Rufus had more than most, but little compared with the wealthy. He felt for the poor, who would eke out supplies and return to their small apartments, many of which had only two rooms at most, which were reserved for sleeping. The rich people had large single-story homes built around an open courtyard, often containing a garden that served as a meeting point.

In the church, however, class disappeared. The upper classes, known as the patricians, and the plebeians, the lower classes, broke bread together, prayed together, and buried their dead together.

That morning, a smaller group of the church met. Only the tested and those who knew about the project attended. They were meeting in the patrician Augustus' *domus*, a large estate nearby. He was well known throughout their district. The home of Augustus comprised several large rooms besides indoor courtyards and gardens. The large central hall where they had gathered now was an atrium. Rufus admired the exquisitely painted walls, sculptures, and statues around the room. The light sprayed through the windows that lined the ceiling's edge.

Rufus had been in several other large homes as a guest of his uncle, who was delivering large orders of meat. Big orders often required Rufus's help. The central atrium of most large homes had the traditional multiple statues of the Roman gods — Apollo, Mars, Neptune, and others — lining walls. These were noticeably missing in Augustus' home.

Rufus had walked fast to arrive on time, and he was out of breath. Joshua greeted him and directed him to the back of the space. Several of the other young men from the project were also there. As they waited, Rufus rubbed his hands together and then down the sides of his robe. He did this several times while looking at his feet. He kicked at the tiles below them. His lips were dry.

John Mark arrived. Several elders entered, and Phoebe came soon after. A handful of other people entered the atrium after her. Mark moved to the front and signaled to the twelve young men, together at the back, to join him. They did, arranging themselves in a line. They stood like soldiers at attention.

"And now your ultimate test is here. If you pass, you may go out and play."

Mark's attempt at humor fell flat in the room. No one laughed. With slight disappointment, Mark cleared his throat and continued.

"Alright, Joab, you may begin. Each of you may follow. Take your time. Please speak clearly so that all of us may hear you, even those who are there in the *triclinium*."

Though smaller, the group still overflowed into the dining room where there were several couches where guests could recline for dinner.

Mark moved to the rear of the room. He joined another man who was holding Mark's scroll. In the weeks since Mark had first brought it to the gathering, it had yellowed a bit, accumulated some dirt along the edges, and had scroll rods added.

Joab stepped forward and began. "The beginning of the gospel of Jesus Christ, the Son of God."

The tones of his voice filled the atrium and spilled into the dining room like a baritone bell. Without hesitation, but with strength, he continued.

"As it is written in Isaiah the prophet."

Rufus shuddered. He glanced sideways at Joab. His mind wandered to a million places — his uncle's butcher shop, the gathering, the plaza, the tentmaker's workshop, the landing on the Tigris where he'd stick his feet into the dirty waters, the room where he slept — this was his home. This exercise of reading what they had memorized was creating a contrast to the sharp tension he was feeling.

Their mission was upon them. He remained exuberant about it, committed to it, and energized by the adventure, the opportunity to see the world, and the chance to share the life-changing stories of Jesus with others. In the same plot where his excitement flourished, feelings of fear were growing as well. He was leaving what he knew well for an unknown length of time.

There was increasing danger in Rome, but he knew Rome. He felt a youthful confidence that he could navigate the trouble of the ensuing threats. However, leaving was dangerous as well. There were many unknown elements ahead. The unfamiliar was ominous. Had the emperor's edict against "Christians" reached other parts of the empire? Would the cargo they carried increase the risk?

Joab finished and stepped back into the row of men. The second man, Tryphosa, looked at Joab, then across to Mark. He stepped forward and recited his section of the parchment. The two men next to Mark held the scroll and were following along.

Tryphosa had dark hair, pulled back tightly, and gathered at the nape of his neck. His olive skin reflected beads of sweat in the rays of sunlight that pushed through the atrium windows. He read smoothly without a glitch.

"And he awoke and rebuked the wind and said to the sea, 'Peace! Be still!' And the wind ceased, and there was a great calm."

Rufus inhaled and pressed deep into Jesus.

"Who then is this, that even the wind and the sea obey him?"

The young man grabbed his ponytail at the back of his head and slid his hand down it. He stepped back into the line. The next fellow stepped up and recited his portion. Rufus calculated the number of guys before it was his turn. Three.

The recitations proceeded. Rufus stepped forward for his turn. As soon as he spoke the first word, the nervousness melted away, and he retold, word for word, everything he had memorized.

Each proceeded until they finished Mark's scroll. From the reaction of the two men holding the scroll, it had been flawless. Mark smiled. He looked less tired for just a moment.

After a slight bit of gaiety, they brought a worktable out into the center of the hall. Mark produced a sheath and from it a knife. The joy dissipated into unease, and everyone watched as Mark took the scroll from his companions and set it on the table. He unrolled it the length of the table.

Everyone turned their attention to the parchment on the worktable. A hush reverberated throughout the hall. Rufus could only hear his heart beating.

John Mark took the knife, bronze with its handle wrapped in leather. With his other hand, he grabbed a short straight board and placed it alongside the first column of writing. He placed the knife next to the board, just above the top edge of the paper. Injecting it into the parchment, he pulled it with quick force toward himself.

A collective sigh released into the room as the people who had been holding their breath exhaled loudly in unison. Mark, too, sighed. After moving the board, he made the next cut. He picked up the piece that the slit had released and handed it to Joab. Joab grasped the *kollema* gingerly. He held it across his palms, lifting it to his eyes. He stared at it, breathing as if to keep his breath from brushing the parchment.

The term *kollema* refers to a single sheet of papyrus out of an assembled scroll. Each scroll comprises *kollemata*, many sheets, that are glued together to create the length of the scroll. It was probably common that a craftsman would make a scroll from twenty of these *kollemata*. The *kollesis* is the joint between *kollemata*, or the place where the individual sheets of a scroll are glued together. Mark had written out the scroll; now he was carving it into newly made *kollemata* to be carried by the men.

One by one, Mark moved the board and cut off each column of the scroll. Man by man, he parsed out the several *kollemata* that made up that man's section. Rufus held five columns, five pieces of parchment. When he received the first, he held it up to the light of the oil lamp. He saw the shadow of a *kollesis*. Rufus moved the arched piece across his hands. He stared at it in awe, seeing the words he'd etched into his brain staring back at him.

"Gentlemen," Mark said, "would you pray with me?"

He covered his head with his shawl. Closing his coffee brown eyes, he reached his arms upward and pushed them towards the ceiling.

"Almighty God, creator of all that is, I sing my overflowing praise and adoration to you. I offer you thanksgiving for the words that you have given me about your beloved Son. I thank you for this tremendous opportunity to proclaim your Son, Jesus, and your Kingdom. And I give you thanks for this group of young men you have given to me who join me on the mission of sharing your gospel with others. May your word go forth to all the nations that many would be free and enter the newness and freedom of your Kingdom."

With that, he bowed his head and lowered his hands.

"Amen." Several of the men repeated, "Amen."

Athos hummed a refrain from the Psalms; the other men hummed along.

JOURNEY BEGINS

John Mark assembled the men in front of the gathering. They stood there — Rufus, Joshua, Artemis, Caleb, Joab, Tryphaena, Tryphosa, Athos, Nathan, Jamin, Lucius, and Marcus — in their belt-wrapped togas. Each man had a canvas satchel slung across his shoulder. Each was smiling, except Artemis. He seemed nervous.

The energy in the cavern was exhilarating. There were more people gathered than usual. Rufus breathed, attentive to the aroma of the spices mixed with the aroma of the burning oil lanterns and the stench of death. He was always ready to leave the catacombs when it was time. Now, the moment's energy delighted him.

"I will never forget," John Mark began, "the day when we left for the first excursion to proclaim the gospel, the one I failed to complete."

Everyone watched Mark and glanced at the twelve.

"I stood behind Paul and Barnabas as Peter spoke to

them. He was grave when he reminded them of Jesus' last words he spoke on Earth.

"I am as serious today as I tell you these words, just as Peter told them to us. Jesus said to them, 'All authority in heaven and on earth has been given to me. Go therefore and make disciples of all nations, baptizing them in the name of the Father and of the Son and of the Holy Spirit, teaching them to observe all that I have commanded you. Behold, I am with you always, to the end of the age.'"

Rufus noticed Artemis had relaxed.

"Through all my failures and subsequent successes which God has kindly orchestrated, I cling to that last, rich promise that he, the Messiah, will be with us always. I hope you will cling to him as you travel to the uttermost regions."

With that, the men knelt. The elders came forward, laying their hands on them. One of them prayed for the men.

"Father, may you bless these men and keep them. Will you make your face to shine upon them and be gracious to them; please lift your countenance upon them and give them your peace. Amen."

As soon as Mark's amen rang out above the rest, the gathering swarmed the twelve with embraces, pats on the back, and smiles. People offered more words of advice. There were affirmations and warnings. There was a glowing enthusiasm for the men and their mission.

The gathering broke bread together and then they scattered in small groups. The men left in groups of three, but they did not return home or to their work; they began their journey.

In four groups, the men travelled the Tigris to the Tyrrhenian Sea. On four separate ships, they rounded the Mediterranean, curving along Sicily and Greece. One ship headed to the port of Pergamon. Two sailed directly to Ephesus, one of them leaving the following day and making a stop near Athens. The ship that Rufus was traveling on made a brief stop in Crete before heading to Ephesus.

A severe storm marked the passage from Crete. Rufus found himself curled up on a bale in the cargo bay, clutching his stomach. Nauseous, dizzy, and cold, Rufus wondered about leaving Rome. Was this what travel adventures were like? This was only his third day out. His physical discomfort was more than anything he'd ever experienced.

"How are you doing?" Joshua had come down to check on him.

Rufus squeezed out a meager response.

"I've never felt so sick in my life. Never."

Joshua nodded.

"Is God indeed with us, Joshua?"

"Here, Rufus, drink some water." Joshua put the canteen to his friend's lips. "I'm sure he's with us. I'm sure he is. Rest, my friend. You will be all right."

It was dark in the ship's belly. Dampness and coolness engulfed the young man. His mind tortured him with thoughts of being abandoned by everyone. First, his mother. His father. Was God even now abandoning him? He felt alone and afraid. He tossed and turned in agony on the bale.

Later, as the nausea eased, Rufus reflected on Mark's story of Jesus on the cross. What was that like for the Messiah? Rufus sensed a moment of empathy, having experienced misery, but none to the extent of Jesus. He recalled Mark's words, "And at the ninth hour Jesus cried out with a loud voice, 'Eloi, Eloi, lema sabachthani?' which means, 'My God, my God, why have you forsaken me?'"

Rufus knew the psalm that Jesus quoted in that moment — a psalm of loss, lament, and anguish. It was a prayer song, an outburst of agony in which the speaker is distressed and pleads with God to intervene. These were the words of King David as he experienced devastation at the hand of his enemies, perhaps when he was fleeing persecution from his son Absalom. The feelings of abandonment were strong; Rufus tasted that now. It is funny how one can savor what is not true and experience it as true. The mind distorts so much.

Rufus prayed the psalm as best as he could in his anguish: "But you, Lord, do not be far off! You, my help, come quickly to my aid! Deliver my soul from the sword, and this sickness. Keep my precious life from the power of the dog! Save me from the mouth of the lion! You have rescued me from the horns of the wild oxen!"

Rufus remembered his skirmishes with the centurion. God was with him. He would be now, as well.

A couple of hours later, Rufus emerged from the hull and rejoined his comrades, who were chatting with the sailors on board. He took a light meal of dried fish and flat bread. He fell asleep against the outside cabin wall.

Hours later, Joshua and Caleb woke him up. "We are entering port. We will disembark soon."

The sleep had served him well. He was almost himself.

They stared at the coastline as the ship floated in. It was unfamiliar terrain, with lighter hues, gentle hills rolling across it, and more barren space.

Rufus released a prayer of gratitude that sprung from his heart. Mark had used the psalm of lament three times to describe Jesus' crucifixion. Now, God had used it in Rufus's life to quell uncertainty and doubt. He still had his garments and belongings. No one had mocked him yet. His companions were here, watching the shore with him. The adventure was beginning, and he burst forth with gratitude.

"I will tell of your name to my brothers; amid the congregation I will praise you. I stand in awe of you, you who are with your people. I will perform my vows. All the ends of the earth shall remember and turn to the Lord, and all the families of the nations shall worship before you. You are king."

EPHESUS

They had disembarked from the boat on the previous day. After a night spent camping on the shoreline, Rufus, Joshua, and Nathan returned to the docks to wait. Another day passed. Late in the afternoon on the third day, a sloop entered the harbor.

"It's them," Rufus said. "I'm sure of it."

Joshua and Rufus made their way to the slip. By the time they reached it, the boat had docked, and its passengers were leaving the ship. They waited until, at last, two figures emerged from the hatch and headed toward the gangplank.

"Artemis," Rufus yelled, "Caleb, we are over here."

The two young men acknowledged them and, clutching their satchels, headed toward Rufus and Joshua. Athos fell in behind. After hugs and adjustments to their loads, the young men took to the road. It was a two-hour walk to Ephesus, the trade center of the economic world. They talked of their journeys on the ships.

"The sailors were so superstitious," Caleb said.

"Yes," Artemis said, "but they opened up to our stories of Jesus. I only hope we planted seeds in their hearts."

"I learned some new tunes from them," Athos said. "It's exciting."

As they neared the city, the roads became stone-paved streets lined with impressive white columns and trees. On each of the columns, the men read inscriptions to many gods — Jupiter, Vesta, Juno, Mars, Mercury, Venus, Neptune, Apollo, Minerva, Ceres, Vulcan, and Diana. This pantheon was familiar to Rufus. His uncle had warned him about the gods of the nations. People should not fear idols because of their power, but because of the illusion of power they had. It tricked men.

Diana, goddess of fertility, was famous. Many who had come to Rome and spoke to the gathering had told tales of the debaucheries at the massive temple of Diana near Ephesus.

They walked down the path; their discussion had changed to theological missives on idolatry and Gentile culture. The building lined street funneled them into the very city-center where a massive area opened. They stared into a large marketplace teeming with people and animals, reverberating with music, bleats, and yells, and wafting with a plethora of aromas from food, waste, and odorous offerings. It shocked the men's senses. Accustomed to the Roman marketplace, this seemed more intense to them. They paused and gawked until people, trying to move past them, pushed them forward.

The market was enormous. It contained many kinds of shops — shops that sold food, spices, shoes, wool, scrolls, and more. Barber shops, blacksmiths, farmers, mercantiles, and more, lined the street. Color saturated the space. Infinite skin tones, a cornucopia of flowers, fruits, and vegetables, and a palette of materials bombarded the men's minds as they beheld a new and larger world. Rome was the center of politics and power, but variety and commerce prevailed here in Ephesus.

Any city-center existed as more than a market. It was a place of business. Artisans created and sold their goods. Business owners made deals. Moneychangers exchanged coins. Their shops surrounded the immense square. Small rooms served as rented space for makers to sell their goods. The person selling them made most of the wares sold in these shops. In Ephesus, however, a class of "middlemen" sold products from around the world.

The plaza piqued their curiosity. Rufus and his companions investigated the sights, sounds, and smells with awe. The square dwarfed his district center and made the Roman Forum seem small.

They passed a lady selling flowers from a stall. Rufus smiled at her as he sniffed a bundle of lavender on her makeshift shelves. He missed Agnus already.

As they glanced around, lapping up the slew of treasures, they saw at the far end a massive structure. Out of the far walls, an amphitheater rose above them with rows and rows of seats.

"That must be the place where Paul caused the riot," Rufus said.

"Oh, yes!"

It loomed prominent in their view.

"Can you imagine?"

The boys stared until Joshua interrupted their gawking.

"We should get something to eat and then follow Aquila's instructions."

They made their way to a smoky booth near the plaza's edge. The men ordered skewers of lamb and paid out a couple of denarii. Next to that stall stood a bakery in the building surrounding the plaza. The smell from the bakery was alluring. Rufus entered and watched as a young girl kneaded the coarse flour and water into cakes, which she patted into circles and threw onto a large hot stone.

Rufus bought six hot cakes for the men. They sat on the ground and ate the meat and bread. The fare served as a pleasant break from the rations on the ship and in their packs. The bread and the meat were chewy. They remained silent as they ate, still eating up the sights and sounds of the merchants and sellers bustling about.

Rufus marveled at the hustle and squall, curious about their lives, their families, their clothing, and more. He also thought with inquisitiveness about their faith. What did they believe? What did they worship? Who were their gods?

"Artemis, what do you think about all those idols?" Rufus asked. Another discussion about idolatry ensued. Artemis talked of the Roman pantheon, and Athos described Greek theology. He talked about how difficult it had been to reframe his thinking as a new believer.

Joshua said, "Israel knew better than to make and worship idols. The Israelites paid dearly for that mistake in the wilderness."

"Yes," Rufus said. "However, instead of manufacturing physical idols out of wood and silver, they have manufactured figurative ones. They bow down not to golden images but to rules and rituals. They are guilty of worshiping human traditions and law instead of the Lawgiver."

Joshua agreed. "Israel had become blind; they turned into the very objects they worshiped."

Nathan said, "The psalmist cried out, 'They have mouths, but do not speak; they have eyes, but do not see; they have ears, but do not hear, nor is there any breath in their mouths. Those who make them become like them, so do all who trust in them.'"

"I wonder what idols I still have in my life, these figurative ones," Rufus said.

"Me, too," Artemis and Athos said in unison.

They finished their feast in silence. But Rufus was anything but calm.

"Let's get going," Rufus said. "We need to find John as soon as we can. I don't know how long it will take us. Any idea where we should begin?"

"It's a long shot, but we should go to the synagogue," Artemis offered. "Someone there would certainly know John. Perhaps they know where we might find him."

"Listen to that! The Gentile tells us to go the synagogue," Joab said.

The others laughed.

"Good idea," said Joshua.

The men gathered their satchels. Rufus asked the merchant who had sold them the meat where they might find the synagogue. He gave them directions. The men moved out of the market on a westerly street. They turned a couple of corners and found a small clay building with Hebrew writing over the mantle of the door.

Joshua entered. Artemis would need to stay out because of his Greek background. Artemis, Caleb, and Rufus waited, leaning against the wall. After a time, Joshua emerged. After grilling Joshua for why he needed the information, a woman inside had provided him with directions to John's district in the city.

After getting turned around and lost twice, the men found their way to the region of the city where John lived.

When they finally found John, he was sitting in a small square on the outskirts of Ephesus. From the garb of the people milling around the plaza, this neighborhood was predominantly Jewish. There were many Jews around, distinguished by their robes, their caps, their hair, and their tasseled shawls.

"Did they know the Messiah?" Rufus thought.

The smells here — roasting herbs, leather, perfumes — reminded him of his childhood when he lived in Judea. That was before his parents left for Rome when he was five.

Rufus immediately recognized the men who were standing with John. They were three of the twelve. The plan was pulling together. Artemis yelled out to one of his friends among the men. The four of them turned to look at the three newcomers. Artemis and his friend hugged each other. He turned and introduced the newcomers to John.

John nodded. He differed from how Rufus had imagined him. He was taller. A bald spot glistened in the sun, surrounded by gray hair. His beard was equally gray, with a dark streak down the middle below his lip. He smiled warmly and gave each young man an embrace.

"Welcome. I'm glad you're here. This is exciting. I'm eager to hear about your journey, but even more so about Mark's work. The other men should arrive from the north in the morning."

It shocked Rufus how openly John talked in the square. This would never have happened in Rome. He wondered why the contrast. Was it a different climate? Or was it just John's confidence?

"We are glad to be here, sir," Joshua said. Then, pointing to his comrades, he added, "And we are glad to see the three of you."

"You must be," John said. "Your undertaking is quite unconventional. Mark's efforts to make a systematic 'life' of the Word, the Messiah, are profound. I am delighted he chose a cohort of young men to bring it to us. I believe it is an invaluable privilege to have a company of fellow soldiers about us, animating and exhorting each other to stand our ground, to keep our ranks, and to follow the author of our salvation, though it be through a sea of blood."

"Follow me," John said.

EPHESIAN GATHERING

everal Ephesian families hosted the men. They believed in Messiah. Rufus and Joshua rested well that night, having unrolled their mats in their host's home. He was an elderly man, a widower, who shared the home with his daughter and her family. His name was Ahkan.

They stayed up late listening to Ahkan's stories about Paul preaching at their synagogue about Jesus. The Spirit compelled the man to believe and follow. Ahkan described difficult times as friends and family rejected him. He shared about the abundance of provision as the gathering in Ephesus grew. Rufus and Joshua, too, were excited to understand what Ahkan had encountered as a believer.

Rufus slept late. John woke him, shaking his side.

"Young man, we received word that the other cohort is approaching the city. Come, we must meet them."

Rufus arose. As quickly as possible, he joined John in the street. Joshua and the other seven had already joined him. They moved up the streets, passing doorway after doorway. The stones in the street thinned, becoming dirt. After they left the city's edge; the road began an ascent.

As Rufus looked ahead to see where the pike was taking them, he could see a small cloud of dust up the side of the hill. A few minutes later, he observed a small group of men descending toward them.

"Look," Rufus said. "That must be them."

The men looked. Within a few minutes, they were embracing each other, making introductions to John, and recounting their trek to that moment.

Turning toward the city, they walked in stride, laughing at the stories and missteps. Joshua told of Rufus's stint in the ship's hull. Rufus took the subsequent ribbing with good humor. Glad to be with the group, belonging grounded him.

It surprised them to be walking together as an entire group. There had only been two times they had all been together since Mark's project had begun.

As they entered the city gates, John raised his hand. The band stopped. With very few words. John split the men into three groups. They entered the city separately, passing an elaborate tent surrounded by soldiers.

As Rufus and his companions passed the door, a

centurion emerged, cursing. He barked orders, and the group of men at his command assembled as one. More orders and they moved as one toward the city-center.

Rufus checked his pulse. His heart was responding to the scare with rapid beats. The men let the soldiers pass. Now, they resumed the way to John's district. There, they rejoined the others.

"Apparently there are disturbances around Ephesus today." The warm glow on John's face became austere. "We must be careful. I suggest you each return to your lodging. Rest. Eat. Tonight, we gather. It will be wonderful to read the writings of Mark. What did you say he called it?"

Joab spoke up, "The gospel of Jesus Christ, the Son of God."

"Ah, the gospel of Jesus Christ, the Son of God," John said. He gazed up. "Yes, Jesus moved about the countryside proclaiming the good news, and we followed."

In an instant, Rufus remembered John had walked with Jesus. He watched John as he paused before them. There was something special in his eyes.

"Ah," he said. "Ah, yes. Go. Get out of here. Rest. We shall hear about this gospel tonight. Your hosts will get you to where you need to be. I am so glad you're here. Grace and peace."

John turned and ambled away across the small plaza. Rufus and Joshua pivoted toward each other. They read each other's mind.

"We don't know how to get to our host's house."

Before their eyes had finished the sentence, Ahkan was standing next to them. He nodded, and they followed him out of the square. Within minutes, they were reclining in the man's home. His daughter had spread a small feast before them. Rufus dove into the barley bread and olives with the haste of a dog chasing a cat.

After resting a bit, they went out and explored parts of the city. They passed the baths and walked through the marketplace.

The library in Ephesus was a huge and beautiful rectangular building, faced with two stories of stunning columns and embellished with curved and triangular pediments that lined the top story of the building. It stunned Rufus and Joshua as they came around the corner, seeing it. The men climbed the ashen white steps and peeked inside the massive doors. They could see multiple shallow, square-backed recesses filled with scrolls from floor to ceiling, towering over the two young men. What they could not see was the system of hallways that surrounded these recesses. Outer walls separated by a narrow ambulatory accommodated the stairs to the galleries. It impressed the men, despite their familiarity with Roman architecture. They had never seen such a collection.

As the evening dropped upon the city and the sky darkened, they returned to the old man's home. They ate a small supper and made preparations to go to the home of Sosthenes. Sosthenes had become a believer some months after the riot in the arena. Now an influential leader in the Ephesian gathering, his choice to follow Jesus cost him his role as the leader of the synagogue.

Rufus had only known one rabbi, the one from his synagogue in Rome — Andrew. Andrew was a good and humble man who had become a follower and fellowshipped in their gathering. He had been fortunate to keep his role in the synagogue. However, recently, a promotion took Andrew to another district in Rome. Rufus wondered about the condition of Andrew's area following the fire and what he might experience in his new life now. It was possible that he was undergoing persecution from his Jewish colleagues and the Roman Guard.

When the men arrived, John introduced them to Sosthenes.

"We will gather in an hour. You are here early because I wanted a chance to meet you."

Kind wrinkles graced the elderly gentleman with a face that found him smiling most of the time. He got right to the meat.

"Do you follow the Messiah?"

A hearty discussion of discipleship instilled in Rufus a familiar tension — both unsure and impassioned. He loved Jesus, but he felt his zeal somehow small and diminished in front of this man who had sacrificed so much.

The hour passed like a quick ocean breeze. As they talked, people entered and seated themselves around the room. Before long, they jammed the space. This was the gathering at Ephesus. Rufus surveyed the crowd with its myriad of faces reflecting such variety and expression.

Worship ensued. It was vibrant and very much like worship in Rome. They partook of the bread and the wine. They sang songs of praise, they prayed, and a couple of people gave testimony to meeting Jesus and believing.

John instructed the young men to come to the front. They lined up; it was like the exam and the commissioning.

As Rufus looked across the unfamiliar faces, he remained curious about the distinct faces he saw — old, young, olive, somber, cappuccino, ashen, smiling, and engaged.

The reading was like the exam, with the exception that each man read from their section of the scroll. They each produced the precious papers and read them to the gathering. The reactions were almost identical to the first time they heard Mark read it in Rome. Sighs, gasps, applause, hallelujahs, and a hush.

Once again, the reading of the gospel had its intended impact on the hearers — first silence and then reaction. Rufus watched as several men discussed among themselves what they received. It took some time scanning the audience to find John.

He, too, was dialoguing with a group near the back of the room.

The talk created a crescendo of sound in the house. John took to waving his arms. Several around him hushed the crowd. He moved up near the young men who had seated themselves against the wall.

"We have received Mark's gospel," John said. "What do you think?"

There was a smattering of responses, mostly positive. Each, however, seemed hesitant to Rufus. None had the enthusiasm that he would have expected, especially considering the initial response that matched those he'd overheard when Mark first read his piece in Rome.

"Perhaps, sir," an elderly woman spoke from the middle of the crowd, "it would be helpful to us to find out what you think of it, Elder John."

"Yes," another man said. "You were with Jesus, our Messiah."

"We want," the first woman said, "to know if this is true — these words."

John smiled.

"Of course, you are right."

The crowd stilled. Rufus rose on his haunches and leaned toward the aging man.

"My good friend, John Mark, has done a marvelous job retelling the story of the Messiah. Inarguably, the Spirit has moved in Mark and his work.

The astonishment of the crowds, the healings, the different people we met, and the demons being cast out — remembering these things has stirred me. Jesus was astounding. It was marvelous to be there when he calmed the seas and fed the masses. He was a startling presence in our lives. Mark has captured well our amazement and our fear.

"Mark was right; we didn't understand. We were slow to comprehend the massive events that were happening in front of us. It was impossible to get our minds around this man. We were trying."

John lowered his head and breathed in. When he looked up again, his eyes held back tears. He looked like he was holding back the flood of Noah.

"Mark is absolutely right," he blurted out with passion. "Messiah's question to us was so important, so very important. 'Who do you say that I am?' Who indeed?"

He stopped again. The room was still as he stood there.

"Mark captured everything that Peter told him. It is a most excellent and most helpful gospel."

The room erupted with delight. The noise increased as many began small conversations of joy and wonder.

John approached the men leaning against the wall. "Who, indeed. Thank you each for your work. Mark would be proud of you. You have served him well. In fact, when things slow down a bit, I intend to write out a similar gospel telling my memories of the Christ.

Perhaps it will be as helpful. Perhaps you will be available to help me proclaim it far and wide."

With that, the men relaxed into the moment. It was the first of what would be many such meetings. It stirred Rufus. He knew his father would have shared his passion, delight, and thrill at this moment.

They slept well that night in Ahkan's care.

SCRIBES

To their surprise, on the following evening, John gathered, from each man, all the pieces of parchment that comprised the twelve sections of the scroll. Rufus had to admit he was nervous about giving them up, even to the venerable John, the Elder.

Rufus surrendered his five pieces to John with a nod.

Artemis also hesitated. He leaned over to Joshua and whispered.

"I'm not sure we should do this."

When John collected them, he handed them to a middle-aged gentleman with a wisp of a beard. With two other men and a stern warning from John, he delivered the parchments into the night.

He said, "You all looked worried. Don't be. Those men are sincere believers and some of the most rugged, reliable men I've ever known. Your parchments will be safe."

John smiled. It didn't erase concern from the men's faces.

"Besides," John added with a brief pause, "I have you!"

They laughed. It was true. The whole point of the work they did to memorize the scroll offered a level of security to the project.

"I assure you we will visit the scribes tomorrow so that you will know what we are up to and that your precious parchments are in expert hands. For now, enjoy some rest. Go check out the city in the morning. You've been courageous in your efforts. There's more to do, but not just yet."

The group disbanded, but Joshua, Rufus, and two others stuck around longer.

"John," Joshua asked, "before we go, tell us more about what it was like to walk with the Messiah."

"You ask that in the past tense. You must mean his time camping with us in his human body. As Mark described, it was astonishing, out and out breathtaking."

Joshua and Rufus looked at each other.

"However," John said, "the question should have been, 'Tell us what it is like to walk with Jesus?' I walk with him today and it's every bit as marvelous now as it ever was. Age and experience continue to illuminate truths about myself that stand in stark contrast to what Jesus wants for me. Slowly, I started believing and then experiencing for myself that whatever future I wanted for myself, I would not find it in my strength. I attempted to dissect my life into 'before' and 'after' Jesus without appreciating the messiness and complexities that such an action would require. Let me say this, reputations are just ugly history in reform. I was a fisherman, now I fish for men. He saved me. He saves me. Every day is living in him. It's amazing."

Rufus sighed hearing this well-known apostle express, without pretense, his travail to follow Messiah. Rufus had assumed it was easy for him because he had journeyed with Jesus.

The following day, they met at the square as the sun stood overhead. John bought the twelve some bread and lamb. They ate together in the shade of an awning. After lunch, they walked to a small building on the outskirts of the district.

They entered a small space. It was lit by at least fifteen lamps. The stench of the burning oil overwhelmed Rufus. Before the young men, a handful of men crowded over two scrolls. Rufus observed that in the middle of the table was the stack of parchments that John had gathered from the men the day before.

"These men," John said, "have the responsibility of copying Mark's gospel onto two new scrolls."

The men followed along as two of the men before them were writing. They were copying the pages onto the new scrolls.

"While those two write, the two men behind each

of them are watching to be sure that they copy it just as Mark wrote it."

Rufus noticed a spot where a word had a line over it, replaced with another word.

"What will they do with these?" Joshua asked.

"Excellent question," John answered. "The first scroll will remain here in Ephesus. People in our fellowship will read and study it often. It will also serve as a template to make a third scroll, which will travel to Jerusalem. I will send the other to nearby cities, towns, and villages where saints gather. They will read it much like you read it to us."

The twelve men discussed among themselves the thoughtfulness of the process.

"Occasionally," John said, "men will read the scroll in various synagogues, hoping it might convince the Jews to believe that Jesus is the Messiah. We will vet these events, recognizing the dangers. However, they will be important to our movement. We must make Jesus known to all."

On the first day of the week, the gathering of Ephesus met again. Enthusiasm and zeal hovered over the assembly as they returned the *kollemata* to the men. Prayers, hugs, goodbyes, and cautions overflowed as the meeting disbanded, and the travelers went on their way to a new city. For the sake of the mission, the young men would repeat the process in several cities, winding their way back to Rome.

THE ROAD

They left Ephesus in their original groups of three. Separated by several hours, they walked along the road talking, praying, and singing as if there were no one around. Rufus's threesome, enlivened by their first presentation, made good time.

The twelve men reconvened in Pergamon. Locating the gathering was much easier in the smaller village. They received a warm welcome from the church, where they called a special meeting to hear the men. They read Mark's scroll just as they had done in Ephesus. And so it went, city to city, winding their way back to Rome.

Traversing the coastline, the men saw Neapolis, Amphipolis, and several other cities. Most often they broke up to move between cities. Occasionally, they traveled together. They read Mark's gospel to as many people as possible. Some asked questions about the unusual ending, but most received it with warmth, enthusiasm, and delight.

Every day, the men talked as they walked. Their successes in Ephesus and a couple of other cities gave their step and voices a buoyancy. They dotted their conversations with humor, which hung playfully over a foundation of sturdy reflection on God, his world, and his Word. Athos would whistle or hum. Often the others would join in if they knew the song. It encouraged them. They began to know each other well.

As they walked, they would banter about things they had seen, theological ideas, the startling growth of the church, and the burdens they carried about their families and friends back in Rome. Rufus worried about how his uncle was doing in his absence. He had hired two new apprentices before Rufus's departure, but there was so much to learn. He thought often about Agnus, missing her.

Meanwhile, Nero's storm — his anger-incited maltreatment of believers — was working its way toward Macedonia. Word of it had reached most of these places. Some had already felt the brunt of the emperor's anger. Mark's words were a challenge and an encouragement to the church.

Rufus spoke often to Joshua and Artemis as they talked about the impact Mark's scroll was having. They shared stories with one another about the people they had met, and the conversations God had permitted with believers and unbelievers. They worked hard, often traveling many miles in a day. Camping was their only option when they weren't being hosted by the gatherings.

They walked the rugged roads, making good progress.

"Rufus, what are you staring at?"

Rufus was gazing from the road across a ravine to a display of small mountains in the distance. Small wisps of clouds stirred elegantly across the green crevasse.

"Do you see that hawk playing on the currents? You never see something like that in Rome unless it's tethered to a falconer at the circus. Isn't she majestic?"

"That she is, my friend." Joshua patted him on the back. "However, we need to stop tarrying if we are going to make it to the village tonight."

"Sometimes I cannot believe that I'm here. I always wanted to see places, and look at this — here we are staring out at this gorgeous landscape, the handiwork of God, watching a hawk play. It's fantastic."

Joshua nodded.

Some days, as they hiked, they would divulge their struggles to one another; other days, they conveyed their joys. When Rufus missed his uncle and Agnus, they encouraged him. When Athos experienced a bout of homesickness, the others came alongside with support, bolstering his teetering faith. Rufus grew more and more confident as the days passed.

"I always felt my mom cooked poorly," Nathan said after several days of camp food. "I would exchange my right arm for some of her food right now."

"You need to save that arm for when you're tempted to sin, my friend." Tryphosa laughed. "You can cut it off then."

Together, they pooled their energy to engage each village with Mark's words. It was the journey of a lifetime, and Rufus was swigging it in as if drawing from a wineskin in the desert. The camaraderie helped because the days were often long, as they logged many miles.

At one point, a man from one of the visited gatherings assisted Joab with a difficulty he was having with his feet. A white circular hardened skin had formed on the soles of his toes, causing great discomfort as he walked. The gentleman removed it by paring away the prominent part of it with a scalpel made of bone. He rubbed it down with a damp cloth and pumice. Joab found great relief in the kindness.

Near the city of Amphipolis, the men, who were all traveling together that day, passed a large hill upon which stood a massive lion. Carved in marble, the white beast, standing erect on four paws, rose above the valley and stared across as if to dare someone to come near.

"That's quite a sight," Nathan said. "I wonder what he's looking at. He looks as if he is guarding a lioness and her cubs."

"I'm not afraid of him," Athos shot back. "I'm a son of the Lion of Judah."

The others laughed.

"You know that part in the gospel?" Artemis asked. They had developed their own shorthand for referring to Mark's scroll. "You know, the part where Jesus sends out the twelve in pairs to proclaim the Kingdom? Joab reads it."

"Yes," Joshua said.

"Did you ever consider how similar it is to what we are doing? I know it's not the same, but we have our satchels and our sandals, and we are going about proclaiming the Kingdom."

"Hmm." Rufus muttered. "You're onto something there."

"We are out here proclaiming the Kingdom's nearness through Mark's word. It's rather amazing."

They all laughed. "Amazing. Astonishing," they exclaimed, mimicking Mark's favorite words.

"Astounding."

"I wonder if Jesus," Rufus said, "was reminding the disciples of the Exodus when he instructed them to take nothing for their journeys. I remember my father rehearsing the story each year when we celebrated the Passover. 'Now you shall eat it in this manner: with your loins girded, your sandals on your feet, and your staff in your hand; and you shall eat it in haste — it is the Lord's Passover.'"

Rufus walked alongside Joshua, who remained quiet, always pondering Rufus's thoughts. The others were still as well.

"Did the disciples understand that Jesus was to be the Passover Lamb" Rufus punctuated his thought with another.

"I'm not sure," Joshua answered.

"Do you think they remembered the miracles of God in the wilderness as Jesus was doing similar things right in front of them? Surely the disciples considered them to be extraordinary moments. When Jesus sent them out, did they have any confidence he would take care of them?"

"Roof, you ask too many questions."

"I agree," added Nathan.

"Here's the ultimate question though: are we convinced God will take care of us on our journey?"

Joshua stopped and looked at Rufus.

"Mark wanted us to. He did. We've come this far."

"Well, at least God and Mark weren't asking us to be like Isaiah. 'Go, and loose the sackcloth from your waist and take off your sandals from your feet.' The last thing I need to do is walk around naked and barefoot. I'm sunburned as it is, and my feet already hurt."

Rufus smiled.

"I'm glad about that."

To himself, Rufus pondered other parts of the Passover story.

"I, the Lord, have led you forty years in the wilderness. Your clothes have not worn out on you, and your sandals have not worn off your feet. You have not eaten bread, and you have not drunk wine or strong drink, that you may know that I am the Lord your God."

Who do you say that I am? Rufus pondered.

Joshua interrupted. "I'm looking at my sandals now, and God, I think I could use your help."

They walked in silence for a distance before one of their companions pointed out a massive waterfall streaming out of the side of a mountain in the distance. It spilled down the valley to the left of the road. The sun shone off the face and sparkled, giving life to the scene before the men. They were nearing the village of Edessa.

BEATEN

After Edessa, the journey continued. They were running low on funds when they reached Apollonia, but the gathering in that city took up a collection for the mission. The generosity they expressed awed Rufus. In fact, generosity had been abundant throughout their travels.

Generosity elevated spirits among the companions as they moved across northern Greece. Eventually, they reached the well-known Thessaloniki. They read the scroll twice there and stayed extra days in the somewhat larger metropolis.

During their stay, the brothers collected the *kollemata* and made another two copies of Mark's scroll. The time of rest was helpful to Rufus. He had grown tired during the last stretch. A couple of days off allowed the men time to rejuvenate.

After the gathering heard Mark's scroll in Thessaloniki, Rufus and the group made their way south and west around the shore, towards the city of

Athens. They were in two groups of six. Rufus and Joshua's group had left half a day before the other. As they approached Chalastra, they met a brigade of Roman soldiers on the road.

They stepped aside as a customary courtesy, in fact, a requirement. As he shifted back, Caleb tripped on a rock along the edge of the road and fell. His satchel dropped off his back and onto the road, spilling out some of its contents, most noticeably several figs and a slab of dried meat. The mishap caught the attention of the centurion. He halted his troop and strutted a straight path to Caleb, who had picked himself up and was brushing himself off.

"You stop right there." The centurion was yelling at Caleb, his veins bursting out below his helmet. Before Caleb had a chance, the soldier grabbed the satchel and scooped up the fallen figs and meat. He threw the figs at a couple of his soldiers and stashed the meat inside his tunic.

Caleb rose to attention off the side of the road. The Centurion grabbed him by the robe. Caleb said nothing. The man threw Caleb's satchel to another legionnaire.

"Search it," he commanded. Turning back toward Caleb, he asked, "What business do you have on this road?"

"I am traveling between Thessaloniki and Larissa with my friends. We each have business in Larissa before we return to our home in Rome."

"What business?" the centurion snapped.

Rufus stepped forward.

"I am a butcher from Rome, and we are searching for different breeds of cattle and sheep to satisfy our customers."

One soldier struck Rufus across the face with the *capulus* of his sword. It stung. Blood splattered out of his cheek. He fell back, catching himself with his left arm.

"Do not talk unless the centurion speaks to you," the soldier said.

Rufus pulled himself off the ground.

Caleb stepped back.

"Search all their packs."

The soldiers grabbed each man's bag off his back. They dumped the contents onto the ground and pawed through the piles.

"Look at this, sir," one soldier said.

Within minutes, they set four of the six stacks of parchments before the centurion.

The centurion stuck the *ferro* of his *gladius* into Rufus's throat.

"What are these, butcher?"

"We are Jews, most of us, and a convert. These are religious texts that we study as we travel. We practice our faith quietly before God."

A thought came to Rufus. "What is truth?" He

had not lied to the centurion, but he had not said everything. What is truth? It was all he had. Was he crossing lines? He didn't have time to reflect on it.

"What do they say, butcher?"

It became clear to the travelers that neither the centurion nor the soldiers could read what they'd discovered.

"They are stories about our God," Rufus said.

"You are under arrest. You are being detained in the name of Caesar Nero."

"Wait," Artemis stepped out from the pack. "I am a Roman citizen."

"We'll see. Bind them. The *legati* and the *legatus Augusti* will be the ones to decide that. Take these men to the *legates* in Chalastra."

They connected the six men in a line. An iron chain bound each one's ankles to the man before and behind him.

As they stumbled to their destination, their guards hounded and ridiculed them, and bystanders on the road taunted them. Except for Artemis, the soldiers struck, tripped, mocked, and whipped the young men. The bleeding on Rufus's cheek slowed.

Upon their arrival at the governor's villa, the centurion escorted the men into the courtyard, where a crowd had already gathered. Something was going on that had the magistrate preoccupied.

The centurion made an inquiry. After an hour had

passed, standing exhausted with onlookers hurling insults their way, they watched as a small man in a white toga with medallions dangling around his neck approached. A conversation ensued between the centurion and the man. After they finished, the man turned to the six men.

"I am *legatus Augusti pro praetore*, the provincial governor of Chalastra and the surrounding region. I report directly to the emperor in Rome. On behalf of Nero, they have charged you as religious zealots causing sedition in the region."

He looked across the group, all the while playing with the gold medallions. He flipped them between his fingers, occasionally scratching his chest with the golden garland along the edge.

"As you can see, I am a busy man. You have two minutes to make your case."

Rufus stepped forward, but Artemis grabbed him and pulled him aside.

"With all reverence, sir," Artemis bowed toward the magistrate, "I am Artemis, son of Ptolemy, a citizen of Rome. I work with this man, Rufus, who is a butcher in the Roman district of Zeno. He serves his uncle there. We are traveling through this region on our way to Larissa. We are seeking cattle for breeding in the *boarium* in Rome. It is true we are pious men, but we are causing no trouble in your area. We are simply passing through."

"A Roman citizen, you say?"

Having accepted Artemis's story, the magistrate turned to the centurion with a scowl.

"Argh, I am too preoccupied to bother with this sort of nonsense."

He turned to the soldiers and, with a sweep of his hand, ordered the prisoners' release. In short order, the guards removed the shackles.

"The normal fine for my court is one thousand *denarii*, but for you gentlemen, it will only be two hundred. You may pay now."

Rufus knew the numbers were fictional, made up to suit the situation. The soldiers, who would split the fine with the magistrate, had tipped the magistrate off as to the resources that were in the young men's bags. They returned their satchels. They each dug into the packs and found their money. Between them, they scraped together the fine.

"I will destroy these parchments so no one can be under their spell. I warn you that the empire does not tolerate religion and rebellion. Now, go."

With that, the soldier pushed the men out into the street and the magistrate returned to the center of his courtyard.

Rufus fell into the dirt. He inhaled, laboring to breathe. His face stung from its wounds. Attempting to focus, he wondered what hurt more, the wounds on his body or losing the parchments.

The others were in various states. Caleb had it the worst. The soldier who was nearest him as they entered the town had flogged him twice. He seemed impatient and pushed Caleb, who led the procession to a faster pace.

Soldiers had hit each of them and roughly searched the men. The centurion had slapped Joshua because his answer to a question didn't satisfy him. The blow left a lengthy gash across his forehead.

It was late in the afternoon. They needed to decide about getting to Larissa.

Unbeknownst to Rufus's group, the other six men had passed through Chalastra while Rufus and his comrades were being interrogated in the magistrate's courtyard.

After some discussion, they sent Joshua to find some food. He was the least ruffled by the incident. The others rested and made a stab at cleaning their wounds. Depression menaced their hearts.

They agreed they would set out immediately for Larissa, knowing they would walk late into the night. They hoped they could reunite with the other pack of men before morning, though they couldn't be sure even where they were. As the men waited for Joshua, Artemis led them in prayer.

Joshua returned with what would have to be dinner, and they walked toward Larissa. Their pace had diminished because of their wounds. They were glad when they saw the moon crest the horizon in front of them. At least they would have light, but they said little.

As they hiked along, Rufus feared the loss of major portions of Mark's scroll. He returned to normal in his head, thinking a thousand thoughts.

"So, this is what it's like to see the world."

"Humans are all the same everywhere."

"Why doesn't God end the Roman rule? It's cancerous for all."

To calm himself, he recited his passage of Mark's gospel.

"For he was teaching his disciples, saying to them. The Son of Man is going to be delivered into the hands of men."

He felt encouraged, but he was also afraid.

THE APPARITION

Before the rooster announced morning, the men arrived in Larissa. It was still and dark.

One lighted window, however, shone among the cottages. On chance, Joshua knocked once with gentle force. After a short delay, the door cracked. It delighted the travelers to be welcomed into a small space where they found their peers reclining around an early breakfast.

Enthusiastic embraces, frantic conversation, and joy soothed a bit of the hurt. Food helped as well, but nothing consoled the deep sense of grief they felt because of the confiscated parchments.

Over the next days, the men recovered, both in body and in spirit. On the Lord's Day, they met with the gathering in Larissa. They recited Mark's scroll to a smaller group, and it went well. For the first time on their journey, four of the men recited their section from memory rather than reading it. Rufus wavered for just a moment on one word, but recovered, and his recitation flowed. As they finished, an elder encouraged them to sit.

With appreciation for the men's sufferings, another elder offered them an exhortation to persevere. With half of them bruised and battered and a third of the scroll gone, they listened.

The elder spoke. "Someone will conquer Rome one day, irrespective of whether the victors are right or wrong to do so. But this triumph will stand very far from the Kingdom of Heaven, as does Rome's current reign. Jesus is King."

Bending forward, he looked deep into each man's eyes and connected. He recited a psalm.

"The Lord says to my Lord, 'Sit at my right hand, until I make your enemies your footstool.'"

Then the elder read several poems from Isaiah's scroll.

"Go on up to a high mountain, O Zion, herald of good news; lift up your voice with strength, O Jerusalem, herald of good news; lift it up, fear not; say to the cities of Judah, 'Behold your God!' Fear not, for I am with you; be not dismayed, for I am your God; I will strengthen you, I will help you, I will uphold you with my righteous right hand."

These words soothed Rufus. His heart calmed. For the first time in hours, he allowed his brain its curious pursuits. He recognized several of the passages from Isaiah's scroll that the elder had woven together. They portrayed Isaiah's confidence that Messiah would befall all enemies — even fear.

The elder read on, "For I, the Lord, your God, hold your right hand; it is I who say to you, 'Fear not, I am the one who helps you.' Fear not, for I am with you; I will bring your offspring from the east, and from the west I will gather you. I will say to the north, give up, and to the south, do not withhold; bring my sons from afar and my daughters from the end of the earth."

The elder paused. It felt eternal as Rufus watched. He remembered looking into both Mark's and John's eyes on different occasions when they, too, misted over.

"You have come from far away," the elder said, "to bring us these precious words about our Messiah. You are a gift to us, and let me remind you — you are part of the Lord's gathering of his children from the ends of the earth. I know it has been difficult for you, and it may continue to be so, but do not be afraid."

He paused once more.

"Isaiah encouraged us. 'Fear not, nor be afraid; have I not told you from of old and declared it? And you are my witnesses! Is there a God besides me? Listen to me, you who know righteousness, the people in whose heart is my law; fear not the reproach of man, nor be dismayed at their reviling; but my righteousness will be forever, and my salvation to all generations.'"

As he closed his recitation, he waved to the back of the room, prompting several women to bring wine and bread.

The elder nodded again. Jamin, one of the twelve companions, recited, from memory, Mark's words.

"And as they were eating, he took bread, and after blessing it broke it and gave it to them, and said, 'Take; this is my body.' And he took a cup, and when he had given thanks, he gave it to them, and they all drank of it. And he said to them, 'This is my blood of the covenant, which is poured out for many. Truly, I say to you, I will not drink again of the fruit of the vine until that day when I drink it new in the Kingdom of God.'"

The women passed the bread and wine. As the slab of flatbread passed, Rufus pulled off a bit and slowly chewed it. As the clay cup was passed, he took a short sip. God was with Israel on the first crossing; he was with his people even now. The cut on his face stung but felt insignificant in the moment's warmth.

The gathering ended with prayers for the men who were leaving at dawn.

After an afternoon of rest and a meal prepared by his host family, Rufus fell into sleep upon settling into his mat. In the night, he stirred at the sound of an approaching storm. Rising from his bed, he saw a fire burning. The thunder roared around him as a heavy rain started. The storm and the fire together combined to create a slush of smells and feelings that scared him.

Amidst the steam ascending from the charred boards, wet by the downpour, Rufus saw a figure. A man approached, somewhat obscured by the ashen air. He reached out and brushed his hand across the cut on Rufus's face.

"Young man, do not fear death," the man said. "Death. The only death to fear is eternal death where you are cut off from the source of life — where you are shut off from God. You, Rufus, are never apart from God's favor, because of me."

Rufus stood awed at the figure before him. The steam gathered and appeared as clouds around his feet.

"Who are you?" Rufus asked.

Daniel's prophecy came to Rufus.

"I saw in the night visions, and behold, with the clouds of heaven there came one like a son of man, and he came to the Ancient of Days and was presented before him."

He couldn't tell if it was audible or just an impression.

With an abrupt eruption deep in his intellect, his passion for Messiah moved him.

The figure spoke to Rufus. "Who do you say that I am?"

An unfamiliar voice spoke out of the haze from behind the man.

"Jesus, the incarnate God, is the Passover lamb, slain on behalf of his people. Jesus is the Way out of the wilderness. Messiah is the promised Truth. Jesus is the Life — in him, the eternal favor of God is present, expressed as the Light of the world."

The voice receded and left a sweltering silence. The form stepped forward.

"Who do you say that I am?" The figure peered into Rufus's eyes.

Rufus looked up. Joshua was shaking him.

"Are you all right, Rufus?" he asked. "Why are you saying that?"

Rufus sat up and shook the grogginess off.

"What, what was I saying? What are you doing? Leave me alone."

"Were you practicing or something? You kept saying, 'Who do you say that I am?' over and over."

Rufus remembered the figure. He couldn't smell smoke. He looked around and discovered his host's home and his mat.

"I must have been dreaming, but it all seemed so real."

"Well, it's time to go. The others will be waiting."

They left Larissa and made a straight path to Thebes, outside of Athens. By breaking up into a foursome, two threesomes, and a pair, leaving at different intervals, they hoped to avoid notice.

For the first time in days, Rufus strode with renewed confidence.

ATHOS

When they met outside of Athens, in Thebes, things were different. Rufus scanned his companions in the mid-morning sunlight. Their robes were shabby and discolored. Joshua's eyes were black and blue. As a group, they were dragging. Their embraces were ginger, tender, and easy. They smiled, but the smiles were no longer boyish grins. Rather, there were mature, wise embers hidden below resolute looks.

Rufus completed his check. Something wasn't right. He looked again.

"Where is Athos?" asked Artemis.

The three men who had been his companions lowered their heads. They said nothing. Joshua looked at Rufus.

"Is he alright?" said Artemis.

Tryphosa looked at Artemis. He paused before tears spilled down his face. Trying to regain his composure, he spoke.

"He's dead."

"What?"

"As we rested yesterday, he meandered away from us in a hamlet north of Thebes. He went to find some food. Apparently, Athos bumped into some Roman soldiers who were in a foul mood. When we found him a couple of hours later, he was on the edge of the marketplace. Someone had beaten him everywhere you can pummel a person. A young woman was trying to attend to his wounds."

Joab continued. "Bystanders told us about the soldiers. Some of them had been milling about the square, complaining about their pay and lodging. They saw Athos as a distraction, someone to bully. They searched him for fun, but when they found his parchments, they took him captive. The bystanders described the gruesome beating."

"I cradled him in my arms," Tryphosa said. "He was on the brink of consciousness. He looked me in the eye. It surprised me how calm he was. Repeatedly, he kept saying, 'Jesus, you are the Christ.'"

With this, Tryphosa broke into sobs.

"Despite our efforts," Joab said, "he died an hour after we found him. Here is his satchel and these are his parchments."

They unwrapped some rags and produced a wad of parchments, mostly charred. A few pieces had recognizable writing on them, but the majority was scorched beyond repair.

In shock and silence, they grieved. No one knew what to say.

The wind blew across the group, stoking their sorrow. The weather was changing. Misty, cold air, foretelling winter's approach. They grieved in silence.

Rufus longed for home and a mouth-watering shard of his uncle's lamb. He shivered. The past couple of weeks had been rough. However, Rufus remained resolute. Despite these having been the toughest days of their journey, Rufus felt assured by the Spirit that the project was worthwhile — that they had been faithful, and the fruits of the mission would flourish.

Simultaneously, a deeper thought brought with it a fog of fresh emotions that troubled his heart.

"Are you afraid of dying?" Agnus's question returned. He missed her.

"Am I?" Rufus thought. "Am I afraid of dying? Was Athos?"

He recalled John Mark leaving the butcher shop, waving goodbye and saying, "Jesus is King." What would he tell these travelers now? How would he find meaning in this senseless beating and horrific outcome?

Again, the Spirit drenched Rufus with assurance from Jesus' teaching that Mark had reported. "If anyone would come after me, let him deny himself and take up his cross and follow me."

With the death of his friend, these words felt more dangerous. They stung, but Rufus leaned in. The implications were extreme. Was this what Mark meant when he said to them, "We are his and share in his suffering and death"? Athos's death cast these thoughts into the realm of another world — a new depth of experience.

The fire of persecution that was emanating out from Rome meant death for many. In this moment, Messiah's resurrection had to be substance enough for Rufus's hope. In death's face, Rufus knew grasping life in Christ was a necessity.

"He is a new creation," Mark said once, speaking of a believer. "With new life in him, he can live in the power of this new life, a life that sees beyond death." These ideas came from Paul and Peter. Rufus believed that Mark's assurance of his union and communion with Christ was the basis for his confidence.

Rufus felt this type of confidence was one thing. "But what about Athos?" Rufus thought. "Athos was no longer here."

Rufus was undergoing a rattling that caused him to sit up and take notice. The young men rested on the side of the road in disbelief. They knew their journey was risky, but no one had expected this. Athos's death stung the young men.

It was, however, Jesus' question that brought Rufus around. He was unnerved and distressed; he was also growing in confidence. Jesus is the Passover lamb and the incarnate King.

Who do you say that I am?

The project must press on, and it would.

"Let's go," Rufus said. Tryphosa nodded in agreement.

The distance between Thebes and Athens was still a day's trek. They walked in silence, brooding over the events of the day. It was nearing nightfall, and they had a couple of miles to walk before reaching the outskirts of Athens.

Suddenly, out of the silence, Nathan burst out in almost a scream. "I can't believe it." He cursed and then said, "I just can't believe Athos is dead."

The men paused with the lowering sun to their left. They each turned toward Nathan. Nathan lowered his head and then his body to the ground. More hush entombed them as they sat on the road to Athens.

"Do you remember the other day," Rufus said, after some time, "when we were comparing ourselves to the disciples with our satchels and our sandals?"

"Yes," several responded.

"Do you remember where that story falls in Mark's scroll?"

"I do," said Marcus. "It's in the section I read."

"Isn't it interesting how Mark talked about the twelve going out and coming back?"

"Yes, but I don't get your point. What's that got to do with Athos's death?"

"Everything, my brothers. Everything." Rufus became animated, standing up under a tree along the thoroughfare. In that moment, a stark contrast to the gloomy pilgrim of an hour earlier spoke.

"What's in the middle of that story, Marcus?"

"Umm. Well, Jesus sends the disciples out, but before they come back, Mark tells the details of John the Baptist's death. It's kind of spooky to be honest."

"My brothers, it just occurred to me how much we truly are like those first twelve, and it is no surprise to Jesus, nor will John Mark be shocked. Why are we?"

"Come on, Rufus," Jamin said. "The last thing we need right now is one of your sermons."

"No, seriously, my friends." Rufus stared them down. "Listen to me; Mark gave us this scroll for a reason. He charged us to take the scroll to others, but he meant it for us as well. And it's now that we need it most. Please listen."

Both Joshua and Nathan nodded permission for Rufus to continue.

Rufus laid out something quite remarkable that none of the men standing there had ever observed. The details of the Baptist's death are sparse, but poignant. Rufus walked through them with his peers. John was handed over to the authorities. His nemesis, Herod's wife, Herodias, seized the opportunity to betray John. Herod, weak and pressured, was more influenced by his party guests than by what is right, and he executed John. Finally, his disciples took him and laid him in a tomb.

"That's the story that Mark embeds in the first missionary endeavors of the Twelve."

Rufus paused unusually long.

"Once again, I am not surprised by Mark's insight. If you will, with John's death as a backdrop, think about Jesus. He was handed over to the authorities. Judas watched for an opportunity to betray him, didn't he? A weak political leader also executed Jesus — a weak political leader pressured by the crowd. Pilot executes Jesus on the cross, and his friends lay him in the tomb."

"That's it!" Nathan said from his seat in the middle of the road. "It's a warning. Mark is cautioning us that, like John, like Jesus, and like Jesus' disciples, there will be hard days ahead, including the risk of death."

"He is," Rufus said. "I'm sure of it."

"I still can't believe Athos is dead," Nathan said.

There was an expectant pause in the conversation. Joshua put his hand on Nathan's shoulder. The men looked down, mostly, at the dirt. Tired and unsettled, they were a sight.

"But you have forgotten the difference between those two stories, Rufus," Tryphaena said, breaking into the pause, "and perhaps the most important point of encouragement."

"What's that?" Joshua asked.

"Unlike John, Jesus rose from the dead. They laid

him in the tomb like John, but he didn't stay there. He's risen. He's alive. Jesus is with us now."

"Tryphaena is right," Rufus said. "Mark is encouraging us. We should be sad, and we should grieve. But if we would come after Jesus, we must deny ourselves, take up the cross and follow him. Our mission is dangerous. We should be careful, but we should also be bold because of our Messiah's resurrection from the dead."

Who do you say that I am? he thought to himself.

Tryphaena hummed. It was a familiar psalm. Joab joined in with words. The men sang together as they moved towards Athens.

ATHENS

Upon arriving in Athens, the group searched for the church. They ran into a believer on the outskirts of the city whom the elders had instructed to watch for them. Word had come to Athens about the itinerant group sharing Mark's gospel. He brought them to the leaders. It was the second day of the week, and after introductions, without pause, Rufus engaged the men.

"We need to begin right now by making a new scroll of Mark's words for you."

Bewildered by the young man's urgency, the elders pressed for explanation. Stories were told about their project, the journey, and losing their companion and much of the scroll. The elders embraced the idea, eager to hear Mark's gospel.

By late afternoon, they had a room, two scrolls, and two scribes. The troop gathered around the scribes and recited Mark's thoughts at a tedious pace. Those who still had parchments produced them for the scribes, simplifying the process.

Joab began.

"The beginning of the gospel of Jesus Christ, the Son of God."

A couple of others read or recited their portion. Rufus recited, Joshua recited, Artemis read. Scribes wrote.

It progressed well until they reached the last words of Artemis, who described Jesus' warnings against the scribes.

"They will receive the greater condemnation."

There was silence — awkward, loaded, painful, still, and charged. Athos was gone, and it was his turn to read.

Then, out of the muteness, Joab spoke.

"And he sat down opposite the treasury and watched the people putting money into the offering box. Many rich people put in sizeable sums."

He paused, and then Joshua continued.

"And a poor widow came and put in two small copper coins, which make a penny."

He went on.

"And he called his disciples to him and said to them, 'Truly, I say to you, this poor widow has put in more than all those who are contributing to the offering box.'"

Rufus said, "'For they all contributed out of their

abundance, but she, out of her poverty, has put in everything she had, all she had to live on.'"

Between them, they delivered all of Athos' section while the scribes recorded it. As they finished, each man stood with tears. Rufus raised his eyebrows, astonished at how much they remembered. The eleven delivered the entire section without missing a beat or a word.

The last men finished their work with the scribes, reading the crucifixion story and the resurrection. By Sabbath evening, there were two scrolls containing Mark's gospel ready for distribution.

As they were leaving, Rufus leaned over to Joshua and said, "Did you feel that?"

"Feel what?" he replied.

"The Spirit."

"Umm!" Joshua's hesitation ignited Rufus's passion.

"Seriously," Rufus said. "Didn't you feel it? I can't exactly give it words. The Spirit was with us as we read. It was as if Mark wrote under God's direction and now, in this moment when Mark's gospel was in danger of being marred, the Spirit came upon us and helped us complete the task. I can't describe it, but I know it."

"God was clearly with us," Artemis spoke. He had overheard Rufus's comments.

On the Lord's Day, the men gathered with the Athenian church. As they had in other cities, they read Mark's words to the church. They had arranged ahead of time for an elder to read Athos' section from the new scroll. Again, God's people received the reading with both hunger and pleasure. It refreshed and revived them.

The next morning, the group purchased passage to Rome on a ship that would leave the following day.

The men agreed to travel together, all eleven of them, despite the risk heading into the fire's center. Nero's persecution was in full swing and was moving into the far-reaching parts of the empire.

They hiked to the market and sought a butcher. After some discussion, they headed to the countryside and found a farmer from whom they purchased a steer using most of their last resources. The bull was brindle-coated, young, and healthy.

"I'm doubtful this is going to be a suitable cover for us," Joshua said as he tugged on the rope to pull the beast along.

"Probably not," said Rufus, "but it will make a fine gift for my uncle."

They laughed.

"I think we should name him," Artemis said. He looked the cow in the face. "How about Athos?"

They broke up in hysterics again. Laughter has a way of easing pain. The grief they experienced reinforced the bond these men shared through many months together.

Moments later, the eleven and Athos entered the market. There, they gathered supplies for the trip to Rome — food, wine, and trinkets to share with their families.

They were going home.

RETURN HOME

The vessel approached the mouth of the Tiber. The men transferred to a small ketch, which took them up the river. Before reaching Tiber Island, the band docked and disembarked.

Joab led them in a prayer of thanksgiving as they huddled together. Tryphosa stepped forward. With resolve, he looked each man in the eyes. He nodded to each of the ten men.

"The world is desperate for more men like you — humble men who are quick to admit fault and slow to defend themselves because they're relying in full on a righteousness and a strength that is not their own. By God's Spirit, you have made your mark. Thank you."

"Hear, hear." The men nodded in agreement.

"You've each impressed me," Joab added. "God has used you in different ways on our journey, and it amazes me. I'll be glad every time I see you around."

Nathan moved forward. "I'm looking forward to

attending the fellowship on the Lord's Day. Until then, you have my greatest respect and appreciation."

There was more approval and agreement among the brothers.

Joshua stepped forward as if he were about to add to Nathan's remark when the clomp, clomp of soldiers' boots echoed into the docks. Without a word, the men split into thin air. It was as if they'd never been there.

Joshua walked away with Rufus by his side and the bull in tow. Stepping aside, they coaxed the animal off the road for a cohort of soldiers marching down the corridor.

As they neared the familiar intersection where, for years, they had separated to go their own ways, Rufus said, "This has been a mighty adventure."

"It has, hasn't it?"

"I love you, Joshua," said Rufus.

"I love you too, Rufus."

They parted company. Passing along the familiar street, the change in Rufus turned the heads of residents in the district. Rufus and his traveling companions couldn't have perceived it because it happened in plodding fashion over many months. Miles on the open road left him tan. His beard had filled out, his hair was much longer with a wave to it, and he had shed ten pounds. He was all muscle.

Rufus made his way first to the plaza. Priscilla's cart wasn't there, but the hunched old man was.

After a brief exchange with the man, Rufus headed to the tentmaker's workshop. He knocked, knowing he didn't need to. It will startle them, he thought with playfulness.

A moment after knocking, the door opened. Agnus stood there, covered in canvas dust. Her disheveled hair tried to hide beneath her scarf. A smudge ran across her left cheek and the shimmer of sweat glistened on her forehead.

Agnus tried to focus her eyes on this man standing before her with a rather large bull behind him. There was a familiarity to this stranger, but what?

Rufus smiled, his heart full of joy and delight at the sight of Agnus's face.

It was then that a bank of memories filled with joy and energy came flooding into her heart. His smile broke the stalemate in her befuddlement. He held out a bouquet of lavender.

Agnus launched at Rufus, squealing. For the first time in many weeks, an embrace was a welcome event. Her grasp was fierce, crushing the lavender between them. It reminded him of the bear hug he had received from John at their first meeting. She didn't let go, nor did he, and the scent of mashed flowers surrounded them.

"Who is it, Agnus?" said Aquila. He came from around the corner and caught sight of Rufus in the grip of his daughter. He stepped back, dumbfounded by the sight. Was this the same young man who had said goodbyes and left almost a year earlier? He seemed ten feet taller than the old man. His tanned skin revealed new muscles and some scars.

"It's Rufus," Agnus cried. She didn't let go. "He's back."

Rufus half waved through the back of Agnus's embrace. A moment later, Priscilla appeared behind the counter.

"What's all the commotion?" she asked. The sight of the young man surprised Priscilla, too. She smiled. "Oh my. Thanks be to God! You have been in our prayers, night and day. Praise Jesus for bringing you back to us. Agnus, let that man breathe."

Agnus released her grip, but not the flood of her heart toward him. You couldn't have etched a finer smile onto her face. Rufus reached up with his hand and wiped away the smudge.

The questions gushed out. Rufus suspected this might happen. He kept his answers short. After about a hundred of them, he waved his arms.

"I must go. It's important to tell my uncle I'm back. I will be back soon enough."

"Don't go," Agnus said.

This time Rufus wanted to stay. It was precious to see her.

"I need to get that bull outside to Uncle Ephron."

Agnus smiled.

"I will return, and we will talk about the future."

Her smile deepened.

The reunion in the butcher's shop was equally emotional. Never had Rufus experienced a squeeze so tight and a glare so penetrating. His uncle was ecstatic. Joy abounded. The brindled steer was a big hit. The stories of where his name came from stung once again, but not as much.

More questions followed. Maybe a bit more detail offered. His uncle made introductions to two new apprentices.

"Do you still have a bed for me?"

"I will always have a bed for you, boy."

Rufus looked at the man with his expanding wrinkles and diminishing hair. It delighted Rufus to hear his uncle in such high spirits. Rufus regretted the amount of fretting he had done concerning his loved ones in Rome. God took care of his own.

After an hour of telling stories to his uncle, the door opened. In walked John Mark.

"I heard the silly scholar has returned," Mark said. Word had reached Mark in lightning fashion, and he sought Rufus.

Rufus received a big smack on each cheek and one of the most genuine, compassionate hugs he'd ever had. Mark looked at him. Their eyes locked. Mark gazed, as if into Rufus's heart. The intensity resonated in Rufus. He felt naked. There was no shame, only truth between two men.

"I am so glad to see you, my friend," Mark said.

"I, too, am delighted to see you." Rufus smiled. "You may change your mind, because I have some questions for you."

Mark howled with delight.

"I thought you might. We will have time for that. Plenty of time."

THE GATHERING

The sect of Jesus — the "Way" — had become the subject of widespread gossip in Rome. Nero persisted in his hatred and persecution of the group. This new offshoot focused on a Jewish carpenter, promoted empire-wide by a Jewish scholar, and popularized by Gentiles. They refused to bend their knees and bow to the emperor or the Roman gods. That Nero hated them wasn't news.

Rufus's uncle explained to him that the persecution had become severe during the time of his journey. Times were hard. Great care was being taken by all. However, more and more Romans were following Jesus. Now that was news.

Several days later, the gathering met in the catacombs. There was a buzz that morning in the fellowship because several more influential citizens had become followers of Jesus.

However, the excitement was eclipsed when people realized that Mark's team had returned and were there with them. The men had arrived one by one for the meeting, receiving an outpouring of salutations and celebrations. The press of the surrounding people with greetings and questions made it impossible for the companions to say hello to each other.

It embarrassed Rufus a bit when the elders invited the eleven men to the front. Mark joined them with a fanfare of his own. He lamented the death of Athos and celebrated his accomplishments. The eleven men linked arms. Mark invited an elder to offer prayers for Athos's mother, father, and sister, who were part of the assembly.

He commended the young men for the mission. Mark joked they had lost his scroll and laughed. He celebrated and declared there were already at least six copies in existence.

"This will be impactful," Mark said.

Rufus cherished Mark's closing comments most of all.

"Men, you're not commodities in God's house," John Mark said. "We love you. You are carriers of his presence. You have done well, and I thank you."

With that, the cavern exploded with applause and thanksgiving to God.

The meeting quieted, and Mark turned to Rufus.

"Rufus, please share a word with us?"

Caught off guard, Rufus stepped forward. One year ago, he would have ducked and hid in the back of the crowd if asked to share something. Today, he spoke.

"It isn't easy to follow Jesus," Rufus said, "and those who do need a deep-seated faith that Jesus was who he said he was." And then, remembering John's exhortation in Ephesus about Jesus and the present tense, Rufus said with emphasis, "Rather, he is who he says that he is.

"Our brother Athos did three things: he denied himself, he took up his cross, and he followed Jesus, his Lord. I will miss him dearly.

"Through our trek, we met many who were strong in their faith despite enduring hardship. The hardships of our journey reinforced our own faith. All our lives are tough. Trends and threats around us can push us toward ambiguity and apathy. We sometimes tend toward a state of doubt or uncertainty. Therefore, we must return over and over to our deep-rooted reliance on Messiah."

Rufus scanned the room. He saw Mark nodding. Joshua was smiling. Joab and Artemis were also nodding. He saw Polonius, his friend, whose eyes were staring as if propped wide open by a board.

"We are living in the new exodus, the one that Isaiah hoped for. Isaiah encouraged God's people repeatedly not to fear. That is why we are so threatening to Nero, and baffling to him and the Roman authorities. We do not fear. Jesus is 'Lord.' No one else could rule over him, and therefore, no one will supersede his authority. Therefore, no one can override his decisions or his impact on our lives."

Rufus paused. He glanced at Agnus and smiled.

"I've said too much. I close with this thought, which bubbled up in my heart after my experiences on this journey. Do you remember how Mark's gospel ends?"

Rufus nodded to Artemis.

Artemis spoke out and once more recited the lines: "And they went out and fled from the tomb, for trembling and astonishment had seized them, and they said nothing to anyone, for they were afraid."

"If," Rufus said, "the glory of God is to reach every land such that they would turn to Jesus and know salvation, it requires his people bearing faithful witness. I believe when Mark wrote for us, he intended for us to experience incredible, unresolved tension between the worldwide proclamation of the good news and the fearful silence of the women."

Rufus remembered the unsettled response on the first night Mark read it.

"If the nations are to hear and more people are to unite in the centurion's confession that Jesus is the Son of God, then we must resist our fear, bear faithful witness, and proclaim the good news. As Jesus said, 'Who do you say that I am?'"

As he closed his thoughts, the movement of a gentleman leaning back at his last words caught Rufus's attention. The man standing near the front looked familiar. Rufus was certain he knew the man. He studied his face closely, looking at the somber blue

218 | THE MARK OF THE BUTCHER'S NEPHEW

eyes and serious look. Why had his words startled him?

Suddenly, fear gripped Rufus. This was the centurion, the one who'd corralled him in the square and harassed Agnus and him as they carted meats to his uncle's customers. He was the one who came to the butcher shop. Without his helmet and armor, he looked different. How could this be?

For the rest of the meeting, Rufus couldn't shake thoughts of the man. The group sang, prayed, and broke bread together. At last, Phoebe closed the meeting with prayer and warned the believers to be cautious on their way home.

Rufus opened his eyes and saw the centurion making his way straight toward him. "Is God testing my 'no fear' comments?" Rufus thought.

Rufus stepped toward the approaching man, who seemed large even without his uniform.

The centurion held out his hand to Rufus. Hesitant but resolute, Rufus grasped the man's hand and shook it with firmness.

"I don't know if you recognize me," the centurion said, "but my name is Vitus."

"We have met. I'm Rufus." He paused. "Why are you here?"

"I have been coming for several weeks. Do you know of Andronicus? He invited me. He told me amazing stories about Jesus and Paul. I was astounded. However, in all honesty, you are the reason I'm here."

Rufus shuddered, wanting to bury himself in the crowd.

"When I confronted you that day in the butcher shop, you asked me to contemplate one thing. You said to consider who I say that the Galilean was. Even more than the question, 'What is truth?' your challenge has troubled me. I have spent many months searching for answers."

Rufus stood dumbfounded by this man telling him this.

"I have looked out there." He waved his hand as if to include the entire universe. "And I have looked in here." He pounded his fist against chest. "That is when I met Andronicus. He has taught me much."

The centurion reached into his robe. Rufus watched as he produced a set of parchments folded along brittle lines. Rufus stared at it as the man handed it to him.

"You may recognize these."

Unfolding it with care, Rufus observed the tattered edges and the bronze-yellow coloring. As he opened the last fold, he recognized the writing. It was *kollemata* from Mark's scroll. Rufus pulled them apart and held them side by side, one in each hand.

The centurion watched as Rufus scanned the documents.

"Do you recognize these?"

Rufus didn't answer. He observed the small, brown

splotch on the bottom of the left parchment — the stain where he had pressed his cut finger on the scroll when the project first began. His mind flashed back to the laughter of that moment. He stared at the pages before him. On the first page, there was a string of words underlined. Rufus looked at it and read, "Who do you say that I am?" It was Jesus' question to Peter.

"How did you come by these?" Rufus looked up at the centurion.

"A soldier under my command won them in a game of dice. I don't see why he accepted these as payment; he can't read. I confiscated them when he returned to the barracks that night."

"Do you understand what these are?" Rufus asked.

"I didn't, but I do now. I took them to my quarters and read them. As soon as I read them, I knew who they were about. I wanted to read more, but I had no access to more, though I searched among the soldiers. I even tried to trace back where they came from. It seems as if soldiers confiscated them in Greece. I imagine the soldiers should have destroyed them, but they didn't. Someone probably nabbed them, thinking they could use them. That's risky business for a soldier, but it's how many of them make ends meet for themselves."

"Chalastra," said Rufus.

"What?"

"The soldiers took them at Chalastra, and, yes, the magistrate ordered them to destroy the documents."

In that moment, two stories began unfolding in that cavern — the story of Rufus's project, arrest, and return, and the story of a centurion who asked, "What is truth?"

Hours later, Rufus's uncle found the two men crouching next to a lantern in the butcher's shop. They talked into the night.

ACKNOWLEDGEMENT

Then he said to them, "These are my words that I spoke to you while I was still with you, that everything written about me in the Law of Moses and the Prophets and the Psalms must be fulfilled." Then he opened their minds to understand the Scriptures, and said to them, "Thus it is written, that the Christ should suffer and on the third day rise from the dead, and that repentance for the forgiveness of sins should be proclaimed in his name to all nations, beginning from Jerusalem. You are witnesses of these things. And behold, I am sending the promise of my Father upon you. But stay in the city until you are clothed with power from on high."
— Luke 24:44-49

This little book has been no small undertaking. I would be remiss to not express my gratitude to the people who have contributed to its release. God has called, gifted, and breathed His Spirit into so many of my friends.

The first time I heard my pastor, Adam Bailie,

speak, he was teaching the Gospel of Mark. It was captivating. I will never forget his sermon about the father, who said, "I believe, help my unbelief." Stefan Wilson continues to connect my thinking to the larger story of what God is doing. I'm glad the Lord trapped his bright mind into this moment of God's "grand story line" as my down-to-earth friend.

Dusty Hart has urged me towards adventure! Without that nudge, I would have never considered pushing this across the finish line. There are a lot of men in my life who keep me grounded. I would live in a cardboard box under a bridge in downtown Tucson if it weren't for them. Thanks John D, Kurt, John T, Bruce, Tim, Jim, Fran, Dean, Mark, Doug, Yvo, Steve, and Jawn [sic].

Thanks to Rod Van Bebber for his input, both stylistic and substantive. It made a difference in the final product. It's amazing how much an editor sees after you have gone over your manuscript a thousand times. Jeannie Wilson offered thorough, clear, and thoughtful insight with a healthy dose of encouragement.

I'm grateful for my family. My mom, sister, and daughter are all avid readers, which inspires me to write better. My brothers are guys who might go on an adventure of epic proportion. I love them all.

Thank you to every one of you who feels slightly slighted for not being included here. You most likely contributed to this project, and I am indeed appreciative.

Finally, thank you Ann for inviting me along this astounding journey through the Gospel of Mark. You have endured my testiness through many great conversations about our amazing Savior. God is graciously changing me. I am blessed to be part of your team.

Oh, and thanks to Jill and the ladies at Christ Church. I am the rich beneficiary of the encouragement you give my wife as she teaches God's Word.

The Mark of the Butcher's Nephew

is a

2021 NaNoWriMo Winner.

ABOUT THE AUTHOR

Jay Flagg

Jay and his wife, Ann, live in Gilbert, Arizona. He is a graduate of the University of Arizona and Fuller Theological Seminary. Jay has written for various small publications and blogs pertaining to men's issues. He is a contributor to the Men's Bible (American Bible  Society). He is the author of The Rattling. His joy-givers include reading, working with wood, camping, and being outside. One of the significant highlights of life currently is being a grandfather to three girls whose high level of energy makes life delightful. One of his favorite George MacDonald quotes is: "As you grow ready for it, somewhere or other you will find what is needful for you in a book."

BOOKS BY THIS AUTHOR

The Rattling

Made in the USA
Monee, IL
15 May 2022

96449764R00142